To Robert (Bud) and Marae Lengtat

and sons Rory, Raymond, and Robert,

for pioneering the introduction of my books

to countless teachers and students

C-140

CONTENTS

Chapter One

VOYAGE INTO TROUBLE

From inside the port terminal building that early Sunday afternoon, Josh Ladd looked through the large plate-glass window as a taxi skidded to a stop at the outside curb. A tall, slender passenger with a full black beard leaped from the backseat. He carried a small bag in one hand. With the other, he shoved some money through the open front window to the driver.

Josh turned to his father seated beside him on the left. "Is that who we're waiting for?"

Mr. Ladd looked over the top of his silver-rimmed half glasses at the arriving stranger. "No, son." Mr. Ladd returned to typing on a battery-operated notebook computer balanced on his lap.

Josh leaned toward his best friend seated to his right. "Dad's secrecy is driving me crazy, and it's about time to sail," Josh whispered. "Why do you suppose he won't say who's going on this trip with us?"

"Beats me," Tank Catlett replied in his slow, easy-going manner. Both boys were twelve. Tank's blond hair, bleached almost white by the sun, contrasted sharply with Josh's dark hair.

"I've got a bad feeling about it," Josh replied.

Tank asked, "How can it be bad to go on a nine-day cruise to the Mexican Riviera, no matter who's with us?"

It was a good question. Josh pondered it while absently watching the bearded stranger dash up to the security officers guarding the door to the large terminal. He showed his papers and was admitted to the room where about 800 passengers were already waiting to board a great white ship docked in San Pedro Harbor near Los Angeles.

Josh absently fingered the video camera that hung from a strap around his neck. He had earlier started to shoot footage, but a security officer had stopped him.

Josh didn't like sitting around. He had barely tolerated yesterday's jet flight from where he lived in Honolulu. After he, his father, and Tank had spent the night at an airport hotel, they had taken a shuttle from Los Angeles to the harbor.

Josh and Tank had explored the terminal, including the immigration section and the agricultural inspection area. They had even ventured into the adjacent room, where several thousand pieces of baggage waited to be loaded onto the ship docked just beyond the back wall.

Now, sitting and waiting for an unknown person or persons to join them, Josh's patience had worn thin, but his anxiety kept rising. He idly noticed the bearded man glance over his shoulder while pushing into the middle of a group of waiting passengers.

Josh's attention was again drawn to the front of the terminal building. Through the plate-glass window, he impatiently watched as another taxi whipped to the curb. A short, stocky man with bright red hair leaped out with his bag. He hurriedly paid the driver and dashed up to the security people.

Josh observed the black-bearded man look back at the new arrival. The bearded one instantly ducked his head and hurried toward the back of the terminal. He paused at a small door marked *Employees Only*. He looked back as the red-haired man entered the building; then the bearded man quickly opened the small door and disappeared through it.

Josh watched the red-haired man moving through the crowd, obviously looking for someone. Josh asked, "Tank, do you see that redheaded man who just came in?" When Tank nodded, Josh continued, "I think he was looking for the bearded man who ducked out that door in back of us."

"So what? We're looking for someone, too."

Before Josh could reply, he again looked through the front window as a third taxi stopped. A big boy stepped to the curb, followed by a younger girl and a woman.

Josh made a strangled sound and gasped, "Oh no!"

Tank absently touched his nose, which was always sunburned and peeling. "What?" he asked.

"You won't believe who got out of that cab!" Josh said in a hoarse croak.

"King Kong!" Tank exclaimed, leaping up in alarm. "What's he doing here?"

Josh had a sudden feeling that he knew the answer. He glanced at his father, who quickly closed his three-pound notebook computer and stood up.

"Come on, boys," he said, starting toward the door as the late arrivals entered. "The Kong family are the people I was expecting."

Josh groaned in anguish. "Dad, you can't mean that!"

"Listen," Mr. Ladd began, "I know that you two have never gotten along with that boy, but . . . "

"Gotten along?" Tank interrupted. "King Kong's the worst bully in Honolulu! He's made life miserable for Josh and me from the day we moved there!"

"I know that," Mr. Ladd replied, still striding toward the newcomers. "But he won the contest my publication sponsored, and the rules allow him to bring his mother. She naturally couldn't leave her daughter behind, so all three of them are my paper's guests."

"But, Dad . . . !"

"No buts about it, son. We're all going to be together on that ship for nine days, so you boys had better make up your minds to get along with one another."

Josh was too sick at heart to reply, but Tank said darkly, "I didn't think Kong could even draw flies, so how could he have won that art contest?"

Josh didn't answer. He was thinking how miserable the cruise to the Mexican Riviera would be with King Kong aboard a ship the length of two football fields.

Tank muttered, "Well, at least he has an even disposition: he's always mad."

Kamuela* Kong had earned the nickname King Kong (which nobody ever dared use to his face) because in size and aggressive attitude he resembled the movie-monster gorilla of the 1930s. Josh knew that, although Kong wasn't quite fourteen yet, he already stood nearly six feet tall and weighed around 200 pounds. He had wide, flaring nostrils, curly black hair, and deep brown eyes.

Josh saw that Kong wore a pair of brown pants and a clean white T-shirt that threatened to burst at the seams because of his massive chest and biceps.

In Honolulu he had always gone barefooted, but now he wore the largest pair of tennis shoes Josh had ever seen. They were obviously brand new.

Tank whispered, "Look at his shoes! They must be at least size thirteen, triple E, in a man's size. I wonder if they lassoed and hog-tied him to get them on."

"Shh!" Mr. Ladd cautioned as they neared the family.

Josh had heard that Ola Kong, a widow, was the only person her son feared, so Josh expected to see a mean-looking woman with a hard face. Instead, he saw that Mrs. Kong was at least six feet tall with attractive features, warm brown eyes, and gray streaks in her black hair. For a big woman, she moved gracefully in a colorful Hawaiian muumuu*.

Mr. Ladd greeted Mrs. Kong and her children, then introduced Josh and Tank.

She smiled at the boys. "It's good to finally get to meet you," she said heartily. "I believe you know my son and daughter from school."

The three boys and Kong's little sister, Kanani, attended the same school near Waikiki* in Honolulu*.

Kanani shyly smiled at Josh and Tank. "Hi," she said softly, trying to hide new braces behind her hand. She was a fifth grader with dark hair, brown eyes, and a shy manner. Her slight build was in sharp contrast to her hulking brother. At school she had no close friends because of her reputation for having a wild imagination and making up weird stories.

Josh and Tank returned Kanani's greeting, then awkwardly nodded to Kong. His huge dark face settled into a disapproving scowl. It was obvious that King Kong didn't relish the idea of being with Josh and Tank any more than they wanted to be with him.

"Hey, haole* boys," Kong greeted them without smiling. "We go holo holo* da kine* beeg boat, yeah?" He spoke in pidgin English*.

Josh and Tank managed to nod without enthusiasm as Mr. Ladd took Mrs. Kong's small bag and asked if she had enjoyed the flight from Honolulu.

"Very much," she replied, "although our plane was delayed in landing and I was fearful that we might miss sailing with you."

"I'm glad you made it," Mr. Ladd said. "I see that everyone else is starting to line up, so we'd better do the same. You'll need to have your passports ready."

They split up, with the Kong family going to the line in front of the counter marked *K*. Tank joined the passengers at the *C* counter as the Ladds approached the *L* line.

Josh complained, "Dad, I wouldn't have come if I had any idea that Kong was going to go along."

"I thought of that," Mr. Ladd replied, pulling his passport from his pocket, "so that's why your mother and I decided not to say anything. We're hoping that this time together will give you boys a chance to get to know each other better, and you will all learn to get along."

"Tank and I *would* get along with him, but Kong won't cooperate. He hates all haoles, especially us."

"Here's your chance to practice loving your neighbor," Mr. Ladd replied.

Josh closed his eyes and fought down a sick feeling, realizing that further protest was useless. He gloomily looked away as the line slowly moved forward. He spotted the red-haired man again. Instead of standing in one of the lines, he wandered around in the luggage drop room.

Josh and Tank had been in that room earlier. They had estimated that at least two thousand pieces of assorted baggage were piled up, waiting to be loaded on a conveyor belt for transfer to the ship, the *Far Horizons.*

Josh watched the red-haired man as he bent to check bags on the outside perimeter. The shipping line had required every passenger to affix a bright green tag, with the person's name and stateroom number on it, to each piece of luggage.

Josh looked back toward the door at the far end of the terminal marked *Employees Only* just as it slowly opened. The tall, slender man with the beard cautiously looked around.

"Son," Mr. Ladd said, "we're next. Do you have your ticket and passport ready to show?"

"Yes, Dad," Josh replied. He forgot about the two mysterious men until he and his father had been cleared to board, been photographed boarding the ship, and joined Tank and the Kong family on the promenade deck*.

Mr. Ladd said, "Mrs. Kong, I've sailed on this ship before, so I'll show you where your stateroom is. We'll pass ours on the way, so, Josh and Tank, you can wait for me there."

Josh had secretly hoped that Kong's cabin was several decks below, but now it was apparent that the boys would run into each other in the corridors of the same deck.

Kanani said, "Mom, is it okay if I stay out here and watch all the people come aboard?"

Mrs. Kong looked questioningly at Mr. Ladd, who asked, "Do you mind her staying alone?"

"She'll be fine," Mrs. Kong replied, then turned to her daughter. "Very well, but stay close. I'll come back for you so you won't have to find our cabin by yourself."

"The stairwell and elevator area is good," Mr. Ladd said. "It's just inside these double doors off this promenade deck. Come on. I'll show you."

Josh and Tank held back, trying to avoid being too close to Kong. But he fell in step behind them, following the adults and Kanani into the ship's interior.

They walked down a long corridor with cabins on either side. Some open doors allowed Josh to see that inside cabins on the right were illuminated only by electric lights. Outside cabins on the left each had large picture windows. Josh knew that outside cabins on some lower decks had only portholes.

"Kong owe you malihinis* beeg," Kong said under his breath.

"You don't owe us anything," Josh replied. "My father owns the tourist newspaper that sponsored the art contest you won. Tank and I had nothing to do with it."

"Aw, Josh," Tank whispered, "let him owe us."

Kong lifted huge fists the size of coconuts. "Kong not owe foh dat," he assured them. "Kong owe you dumb haoles punch in da face foh da times you get away from Kong back in Hawaii."

Tank groaned and Josh gulped, glancing hopefully at the adults, but they didn't seem to have overheard the threat. Instead, they stopped in the stairwell area.

"Kanani should be okay here for awhile," Mr. Ladd said, pointing to the open area with elevators facing the wide stairwell.

One set of wide steps led to an upper deck and another set led down. There were a couple of potted palms and two comfortable chairs on each side of the area. Large picture windows allowed a view of the harbor on one side and the docks on the other.

Mr. Ladd said, "Now, Kanani, please be careful when the porters start bringing the baggage up on the elevators. In the past, they've set the bags in this area before taking them to the individual staterooms."

"I'll be careful," Kanani replied. She glanced around, then pointed. "I'll take that chair over there by the window so I can watch the other boats going by."

When Kanani had settled herself, half hidden by a potted palm tree about six feet high, Josh followed the rest of his party down the corridor. His feet seemed to drag, knowing what miserable days lay ahead.

* * *

Kanani watched the others leave. She was glad to be alone. Now she could indulge in her favorite pastime of making up stories about what went on around her.

The last few passengers had boarded and moved down the outside deck or taken the stairs up or down to other decks. Kanani, who had just turned twelve, watched the elevators open. Two dark-skinned young men in gray tunics began unloading baggage. In moments, bags of all shapes and sizes partially filled the stairwell area. The men reentered the elevators, and the doors closed. Kanani closed her eyes and began to imagine.

The elevators really are secret rocket ships, she decided. *They could go up through the top deck of the ship and off to the stars, but the men handling the baggage don't know that. If I could . . .*

Kanani broke off her musing at the sound of a suitcase being unzipped. She opened her eyes to see a tall, bearded man bending over a bag.

He glanced furtively around the silent stairwell area, then reached into his pants pocket and took out a penknife. With it, he made a small cut in the top seam of the bag's lining. After another quick look around, he retrieved a small, flat package from his coat pocket.

He shoved the black package into the cut lining and pulled a roll of clear mending tape from his pocket. He tore off a piece of tape, sealed the cut, and started to zip the bag closed. Suddenly, he tensed, whirling around to look up the wide stairs.

Hastily, he slid the knife into his pocket and quickly examined the shipping line's identification tag. Then he rushed through the outside doors onto the promenade deck.

Seconds later, a short, stocky, red-haired man ran down the stairs. He glanced around the stairwell area and saw Kanani. Breathlessly, he asked, "Did you see a bearded man come through here a moment ago?"

She nodded and pointed. "He went that way."

"Thanks." The red-haired man rushed outside.

Kanani's imagination took wings. *The one with the beard looks like a man, but he's really an alien from outer space. The redheaded one is the only person who knows that the alien has hidden a deadly secret formula in that bag. But the owner doesn't know that, so he could be in terrible danger.*

Kanani walked over to the bag and lifted the identification tag.

It read: *Josh Ladd, Stateroom #7026.*

Chapter Two

A GIRL'S SECRET

Kanani stared at Josh's bag, trying to decide what to do. She was so deep in thought that she didn't hear anyone approach until someone spoke from behind her.

"Hi."

Kanani spun around to see a short, plump girl wearing wire-rimmed glasses.

"I didn't mean to scare you," the girl said with a friendly smile. "My name's Vicki Fyfe. I saw you in the terminal. I think we're the only girls our age on this whole big ship."

Vicki spoke in short, breathless bursts, as though she were afraid of being interrupted before she could finish. "I'm eleven and in the fifth grade at Modesto, California. I'm with my mom. Dad's in the air force overseas. This is my first cruise. Where are you from?"

Kanani wanted to draw back from this gushing girl, but didn't like not having any girls her age around for a week. Kanani decided to be friendly to Vicki. "Hi, I'm Kanani Kong from Waikiki . . . "

"Waikiki, Hawaii?" Vicki interrupted with a delighted

squeal and a clap of her hands. "I've never been there, although I always wanted to. Let's go on deck and watch our ship leave. Then you can tell me about it."

Kanani hesitated. "I can't. I told my mother and brother I'd wait here."

"Do you know your cabin number?"

"Yes. Why?"

"Then, let's go there and tell your mother that we're going up on deck. That will be okay, won't it?"

Nodding, Kanani glanced down at Josh's bag and then toward the outside double doors where the two mysterious strangers had gone. "I guess so. But first, there's something I need to tell somebody."

"Can't it wait?" Vicki cried, eyes bright through her glasses. "I want us to be friends right away."

Kanani thought fast. Nobody knew she had seen the bearded man hide something in Josh's bag. *He probably won't be in any danger for awhile,* she decided. "Okay, Vicki, let's go find my mom."

* * *

While Mr. Ladd showed the Kongs to their stateroom, Josh and Tank entered theirs. There was a small entryway with a large poster showing how to put on a life jacket and the location of the cabin's lifeboat station. The bathroom was immediately to the left, with a closet just beyond that. From there, the room widened out to show two narrow beds, a dresser with a large mirror, a television set, and a chair supported by a wide base.

"Your dad will need one bed, so that means either you or I will have to sleep on the floor," Tank complained, glancing past the beds to the three-foot wide window that looked onto the promenade deck.

Josh shook his head and pointed to the wall over the left-hand bed. "There's a hidden one up there that pulls down." He glanced down at the video camera slung around his neck on a wide strap. "I should shoot some footage, but I'm still so upset about Kong being on board that I don't feel like it. I wish I hadn't come."

"Me, too." Tank walked over to the picture window. It was tinted so cabin occupants could look out, but people passing on the promenade deck couldn't see in.

Josh complained, "A whole nine days on a ship with the one person in the world who makes our lives miserable! And he's already made a threat . . . "

Josh broke off as someone knocked on the stateroom door. Josh took a few quick steps and opened it. A nice-looking black man stood there.

He smiled and extended his right hand. "Welcome aboard, mon." He had a slight Jamaican accent. "I'm Erek, your cabin steward. I'm here to make your trip as comfortable as possible. Call if you need anything."

"Thanks. I'm Josh Ladd. He's Tank Catlett. My dad will be along soon."

"You can do something for me," Tank said, also shaking hands with the steward. "Show me how we can get that bed out of the wall."

Erek entered the room and closed the door. "You don't have to think about that because I'll make up your beds each night while you're at dinner," he explained. "Now, let me show you where the life jackets are . . . "

He broke off when there was a knock at the door. Josh opened the door to see a brown-skinned man carrying several bags.

Josh recognized the luggage and pointed to the closet. "Please put them in there."

The porter obeyed, then left while Erek showed the boys where the life jackets were stowed under the beds, and how to get to their lifeboat station for the mandatory drill, which would be announced.

After Erek departed, Josh laid the video camera on the left-hand bed. "I guess we may as well unpack," he said to Tank.

"Yeah, I guess so," Tank replied glumly. He lifted his large blue-black bag onto the right-hand bed and began opening it.

Josh reached behind his father's two large gray bags and hoisted his beige one onto the bed beside his camera. "Mine's partly open," he commented, eyeing the zipper.

"The agricultural inspectors in the terminal probably did it," Tank replied.

"I thought they checked baggage only coming into port, not going out," Josh answered. "Oh, well." He shrugged, unzipped the bag the rest of the way, and began unpacking.

When both boys had hung up their clothes and put their socks and underwear into drawers, Josh shoved his empty bag to the back of the closet behind Tank's.

"Come on, Tank," Josh said, picking up his video camera. "Let's go on deck and watch the ship leave."

As the boys left the stateroom and hurried to the left, the tall man with the black beard watched them from the far right end of the corridor. When Josh and Tank turned the corner and were lost to sight, the man walked rapidly toward the cabin the boys had just vacated.

* * *

Kanani and Vicki met Mr. Ladd carrying his notebook computer down the corridor a few doors from where he had left the Kongs' stateroom.

"Hello again, Kanani," Mr. Ladd greeted her. "I see you've already made a new friend."

"Yes. Her name's Vicki." Kanani turned to the other girl. "He's Mr. Ladd."

"Hi, Mr. Ladd. My father's in the air force. What do you do?"

"I publish a tourist periodical in Waikiki. Kanani's big brother won an art contest that we sponsored, so he got this free trip and brought his mother and Kanani along."

Vicki let out a delighted squeal. "Oh, how wonderful! My mom and I saved for years to make this trip. Kanani, I have to meet your brother. He must be very talented. I can't even draw a straight line."

Kanani squirmed uncomfortably and lowered her eyes. Mr. Ladd chuckled. "You'll find him and Mrs. Kong in that third cabin on the left. Well, nice meeting you, Vicki. See you later, Kanani."

Mr. Ladd strode off on long legs while the girls continued

toward the Kongs' cabin. Vicki chattered cheerfully about what a lucky girl Kanani was and how she wished she had a brother, but she was an only child.

Vicki abruptly broke off her flow of words and frowned at her newfound friend. "What's the matter, Kanani? Why are you so quiet?"

"No reason," Kanani replied with a sigh. Then she stopped and turned to face Vicki. "Well, yes, there is. But I can't talk about it."

"Why not? Is it a secret?"

Kanani nodded without speaking.

"Oh, I love secrets! Tell me, please! I won't tell."

Kanani hesitated, torn between wanting to share what she knew, but fearful that Vicki would be like all the other girls and eventually not be her friend anymore. It was hard not to be popular, and it was especially hard to tell anyone what she had heard other kids at school say when they thought she couldn't hear.

"Kanani?" Vicki's voice had a question in it.

"Huh?" Kanani looked up. "What?"

"Weren't you listening? I said, 'If you tell me a secret, I'll tell you one.' So how about it?"

Licking her lips, Kanani debated, her thoughts in a turmoil. If she mentioned an alien, Vicki would act like other girls and leave. But if Kanani only told part of what she had seen . . .

"Well?" Vicki said.

"Promise you won't tell?" Kanani asked.

"Promise!"

Kanani glanced around, then leaned closer to Vicki and said in a low voice, "I saw something . . . "

Mrs. Kong opened the cabin door, breaking into her sentence. "Oh, there you are, Kanani. Come in and see our cabin, and then let's all go on deck and watch the ship leave. Bring your friend with you."

"In a minute, Mom," Kanani replied.

When Mrs. Kong had closed the stateroom door, Vicki turned eagerly to Kanani. "What did you see?"

"Shh! Tell you later."

"I can hardly wait!" Vicki exclaimed.

* * *

Josh stood near the front of the promenade deck with his father, Tank, and a number of other passengers. They lined the rail as a deep-throated blast of the ship's whistle announced imminent departure. Josh leaned over the polished dark wooden rail and began shooting footage as the *Far Horizons* eased away from the dock.

Mr. Ladd said, "I think Mrs. Kong is a fine woman. Her daughter seems nice, too. Now, as to her son . . . "

"Don't mention him!" Tank said with a mock groan.

"Just the same," Josh's father continued, "I'm satisfied that Mrs. Kong doesn't want you three boys getting into any trouble. I heard her tell Kamuela that he was to be polite to you two, just as I've already told you to be nice to him."

"Aw, Dad," Josh protested, turning off the video camera and facing his father. "You don't know Kong! Why, a while ago when you and his mother were talking, Kong threatened

Tank and me, saying he could hardly wait to get us alone to punch us out."

"He was just bluffing," Mr. Ladd replied.

"I don't think so," Josh said.

"Me, either," Tank added.

"Boys, you both know what the Bible says about loving your enemies. Now here's your chance to practice what you believe."

"We're willing, Dad," Josh said, "but Kong won't let us."

"Try," Mr. Ladd said firmly.

Moments later, Mrs. Kong and her family approached with Mrs. Fyfe and her daughter, Vicki.

After acknowledging Mrs. Kong's introductions, Josh excused himself, saying he had to shoot some video footage of the ship getting under way. Tank went along.

As the friends squeezed in among other passengers so Josh could get to the rail, he told Tank to keep an eye on Kong. Josh didn't want him sneaking up on him while his eye was pressed to the viewfinder.

The ship cleared the harbor and turned south on the open Pacific, and Tank moved back toward Mr. Ladd and the two women. The girls and Kong had wandered off.

Josh stayed where he was, fighting to keep his feelings about Kong from showing.

I've tried every way I can to get along with him, Josh told himself. *I don't want trouble with him, but he keeps forcing it on me. Now we have to spend all our time on this ship, where we'll see each other every day.*

Josh's eye was on the viewfinder, tracking an incoming freighter, when he heard someone coming up fast behind him. Josh whirled around just as Kong's mammoth foot smashed down on Josh's toes.

"Ouch!" Josh cried. "You did that on purpose!"

Kong sneered, "You got da kine warning. Kong see you, Kong hurt you. An' stay away da kine sistah*! No talk to Kanani, yeah?" Without waiting for an answer, Kong shuffled ponderously down the deck.

Tank came hurrying back. Josh quickly repeated what Kong had said.

Tank exclaimed, "He's just looking for any excuse to beat up on us!"

Josh sighed heavily. "I guess all we can do is to try to stay away from Kanani and out of Kong's way."

"That won't be easy. I just overheard your father telling Mrs. Kong that her family will be at our table for meals."

Josh closed his eyes as though in real pain. "How much worse can things get?"

A few minutes later, when Mr. Ladd had left Mrs. Kong and rejoined the boys, Josh asked if it was true about having the Kongs at their table.

"Yes, of course," Mr. Ladd replied. "Now, we'd better return to our stateroom so I can unpack."

As Josh and Tank followed Mr. Ladd into the ship, Josh asked, "Dad, do we really have to eat with Kong?"

"Yes, we do. The Kongs are the newspaper's guests, so naturally they take their meals with us. I've also asked the maitre d'* to seat us at a table for eight so the Fyfes can join us. The girls are becoming friends."

Josh and Tank exchanged painful glances while they continued toward their cabin. Mr. Ladd explained that the ship's policy required assigned seating at lunch and dinner. Only at breakfast was there open seating in which passengers might sit anywhere they wanted. One option was a buffet-style breakfast at the stern of an open deck.

Approaching their stateroom, Josh saw Erek leaving it. Josh introduced his father to the steward.

"You're Mr. Ladd?" Erek asked in obvious surprise while shaking hands. When Mr. Ladd nodded, Erek cried, "Oh, mon! Then, who was that mon who said he was you?"

"What man?" Josh's father asked.

"One with a beard. He was here a few minutes ago. He told me that he was you and had misplaced his key. So I let him into your stateroom."

"Uh-oh!" Josh cried. "Dad, something's wrong!"

Chapter Three

TRAILING A MYSTERY MAN

Mr. Ladd quickly inserted his key into the lock. "Let's find out what's going on," he said, pushing the stateroom door open.

Josh followed his father into the cabin, with Tank and Erek trailing behind. A quick look showed that nobody else was there.

Mr. Ladd said crisply, "Boys, check your clothes and personal belongings." As they hurriedly obeyed, Mr. Ladd put his computer on the right-hand bed and reached for his suitcases.

While Josh and the others examined their belongings, Erek apologized for letting anyone in. Mr. Ladd assured the steward that it wasn't his fault; he had no way of knowing that the intruder wasn't who he said he was.

Josh ran his hands gently over the clothes he had hung up. "Everything's here, Dad," he announced.

"Same here," Tank added.

Mr. Ladd said, "Nothing of mine seems to be missing, either."

Josh said, "Tank, maybe we'd better check our bags."

"Why?" Tank asked. "We emptied them just a little while ago, and you can see that they're in the closet."

22

Josh nodded. "That's right. Dad, why did someone want to get into our cabin?"

"I don't know," Mr. Ladd replied, turning to Erek. "But there's no harm done. However, maybe you'd better tell me what this man looked like."

The steward answered, "He was about as tall as me, but thinner and had a full dark beard."

"Dad!" Josh exclaimed. "I just thought of something." Josh briefly told his father about seeing a man answering that description in the terminal. He recalled seeing the second man with the red hair coming into the terminal and the bearded man ducking into an *Employees Only* door.

"The last I saw of him," Josh concluded, "was when he came out that door just as it was my turn to show my passport. I don't know what happened to the other man."

"Well," Mr. Ladd replied, "I guess it was just a mistake, because there's nothing in this cabin that he could possibly want. So let's just forget about it."

Josh watched his father and Erek walking down the corridor together. "I hope Dad's right," Josh told Tank, "but I thought there was something strange going on when I saw those two men in the terminal. Now I'm sure of it."

* * *

Darkness had replaced the sunset, and all the other passengers except Kanani and Vicki had left the deck. The two girls stood alone at the ship's port* bow* rail. Vicki reminded Kanani, "You were going to tell me a secret."

Kanani didn't want her newfound friend to think of her as

strange, as her classmates did in Hawaii. She decided not to tell Vicki her idea about an alien hiding something in Josh's luggage. She would make her story more believable.

"A while ago," Kanani said, lowering her voice, "down by the elevators, I saw a man put something in a suitcase that wasn't his."

"Why would he do that?"

"I think he had to hide it real fast because he's a crook, and a private detective was closing in on him. Or maybe it was a government agent. That's it! A detective wouldn't follow somebody out of the United States, so he must be a secret government agent."

"Really?" Vicki's eyes lit up. "What was hidden?"

Kanani, pleased that her imagination had created a believable story, answered, "I couldn't see, except it wasn't big. It had to be very valuable to risk hiding it in a stranger's bag."

Kanani told how the stocky man with red hair had asked if she had seen the bearded man. "After they were gone," Kanani concluded, "I checked to see who owned the bag in which something was hidden. It's Josh Ladd's."

"The same Josh Ladd I just met?"

"The same. And you know what else? I'll bet Josh doesn't know it."

"Are you going to tell him?"

"Yes, because he could be in danger."

"He could? Why?"

"Because the crook has to get back whatever he hid in that bag, so he must have memorized the name and cabin number on the tag. But if Josh finds it first . . . "

Vicki interrupted. "Oh, I see. Yes, that would be terrible! Let's go find him and tell him right now."

A series of melodic gongs sounded, and the public-address system announced that dinner was served in the dining room. "I'll have to wait until Josh is alone," Kanani decided.

She and Vicki checked a large wall diagram under glass showing the location of various places on each deck. They had just located the dining room on the chart when Kanani saw Josh and Tank reflected in the glass. They were among a group of fifty or so other passengers going up the wide stairs.

Kanani whispered, "Look! The boys must be going to dinner, too. Come on. Now's my chance to tell Josh. Would you get Tank away so I can tell Josh alone?"

"Of course! Oh, this is so exciting!"

* * *

Josh hadn't seen the girls until Tank nudged him.

"Don't look now, but Kanani is coming toward us with Vicki."

"Hurry up, Tank," Josh urged, quickening his stride. "Let's not give Kong any excuse to beat on us."

"Yeah," Tank agreed glumly. "Kanani's the one person in this world that Kong likes. And we promised your dad we'd keep out of trouble with Kong."

The boys mingled with the adult passengers until they arrived at the assigned round table for eight. It was covered with a neat white tablecloth and located next to a large window. It overlooked the ocean, which was no longer visible because darkness had fallen.

Josh's father was already at the table with Mrs. Kong, Mrs. Fyfe, and Kong. Kong scowled across the large table at the boys just as Kanani and Vicki arrived.

Josh wanted to sit between his father and Tank, far away from Kong and Kanani, but Vicki surprised Josh by suddenly seating herself to his left. This forced Tank to take the chair to Mr. Ladd's right.

The dining room steward handed everyone large menus while the busboy poured water into tall glasses.

Vicki leaned close to Josh. From behind her menu, she whispered, "Kanani must talk to you real soon."

"Oh?"

Vicki nodded. "Yes, you see . . . "

Mr. Ladd interrupted by clearing his throat and raising his voice slightly to be heard above the hubbub of several hundred other diners. "In our home, it's customary to ask God's blessing on our meals. Would it be agreeable with all of you if I say grace?"

Sometimes Josh was uncomfortable with his father's ritual. Josh preferred that anyone who wanted could pray silently. But with the trouble Josh foresaw on this cruise, he was grateful when the two women approved.

Mr. Ladd bowed his head and prayed, "O God, thank you for this food, and we ask you to give us all a safe voyage."

Josh then stared thoughtfully at the wide array of silverware around his plate. He tried to remember what his father had told him. Instead of a simple knife, fork, and spoon, this ship served

European style. That meant there were three forks to the left of the plate, two knives and two spoons on the right, and a small fork at the top of the plate.

But Josh's thoughts were on what Vicki had whispered. He tried to think how he could possibly keep from having to talk to Kanani.

From behind her menu, Vicki whispered to Josh, "You had better see Kanani alone real soon because you could be in danger."

That captured Josh's attention, but he thought, *And I'll be in real trouble from Kong if I speak to Kanani.* He asked Vicki, "How could that be?"

"Shh!" she warned, glancing furtively around. "You have something somebody wants."

"What?"

"Oh, you don't know about it. The man with the beard has to get it back, but he's being chased . . . "

Josh interrupted. "A man with a black beard?" His tone was harsh as he recalled the man's strange behavior in the terminal and how he had lied to Erek to get into the Ladds' stateroom.

"Yes," Vicki assured him, "and if he can't get back what you have . . . "

Josh interrupted. "I haven't even been near that man, so how could I have anything of his?"

"I can't say anything more," Vicki replied. "Kanani will tell you the rest."

Josh felt anxiety start to build, knowing that Kong had

warned him to stay away from his sister. But Josh was curious about what Kanani wanted to tell him.

His thoughts were interrupted by his father asking, "Son, have you decided what to order?"

Josh forced himself to concentrate on the printed words before him. He had never seen such a selection. There were appetizers, soups, salads, and entrées, plus cheeses and desserts. Josh glanced at his dad, knowing he would try to subtly give more-inexperienced diners some guidelines.

"Ladies," he began, looking across at Mrs. Kong and Mrs. Fyfe, "I love escargot* as an appetizer, but I find caviar* too salty. Do you agree?"

Josh thought he saw Kong's mother give a small sigh of relief, and Mrs. Fyfe nodded. Josh also felt more relaxed, for he had thought of ordering the escargot, but he had forgotten that the final *t* was silent. He would have mispronounced it and been embarrassed.

"Sometimes my wife asks me to order for her," Mr. Ladd continued. "Mrs. Kong, if you'd like, I would be happy to do that for you."

"Mahalo*," she replied. "Please do."

Josh saw his father look at Vicki's mother, but she was obviously more sophisticated. She said quickly, "I believe I'll have the apricot nectar, but no soup or salad. I'll decide on the entrée later."

Josh tried to concentrate on ordering when the dining room steward came to him, but his mind was still occupied with Vicki's ominous words. He ordered tomato juice as an appetizer, cream of asparagus soup, and hearts of lettuce with carrot curls salad. For his entrée he chose broiled prime sir-loin steak with Bernaise sauce. For dessert he ordered Black Forest cake with a glass of milk. He then fell silent while the others at the table conversed freely. Josh wanted very much to talk with Tank, but it was impossible because Mr. Ladd sat between them.

Josh absently picked at his food, drawing some satisfaction only from watching Kong. It was obvious that he had never eaten in anything fancier than a fast-food restaurant.

When Kong's escargot came, instead of reaching for the small appetizer fork at the top of the plate, he picked up the dinner fork nearest the plate. He speared one of the small, highly seasoned snails and chewed with his mouth open.

"Good!" he announced, stabbing at another.

Josh was tempted to inform Kong that he was eating snails, but Josh knew that he didn't dare for fear that Kong might just spit it out. That was because snails in Hawaii were six inches long and definitely not edible.

Josh kept silent and watched as Kong picked up any knife or fork as the steward served new dishes. Josh kept his eyes on his father and imitated him, choosing the same piece of sil-verware he did.

Nothing could long keep Josh's mind from returning to Vicki's warning. He tried to draw her into conversation again, but she kept talking to Kanani.

Josh was finishing his dessert when Tank leaned back in his chair and motioned behind Mr. Ladd's back.

Tank jerked his head and swept his eyes across the huge dining room. Josh followed them to where Tank's gaze rested on a man sitting alone at a table for two. His back was to Josh, but Josh could see the right side of the man's face. He had a full dark beard.

As Josh watched, wondering who the man was and why he had lied to get into the Ladds' stateroom, the stranger wiped his mouth with the napkin and stood.

Josh suddenly realized there was a way to find out the man's name. By following him to his stateroom, Josh could get the cabin number. He had learned from his father that the ship published a passenger list with stateroom numbers. If Josh knew the bearded man's number, he could look up his name.

"Uh, Dad," Josh said with sudden resolve, "may I please be excused?"

His father looked at him with obvious surprise. "If you feel it's necessary, son."

"It's necessary," Josh replied hurriedly, dropping his napkin on the table and standing up.

"Me, too," Tank said, doing the same.

Josh saw the questioning look in his father's eyes, but that didn't matter. Josh and Tank began dodging and weaving their way through the many stewards and busboys. Josh and Tank kept the stranger in sight as he exited the dining room.

Tank warned, "Don't lose sight of him."

"I'm trying, but we don't want him to see us. Wait'll I tell you what Vicki told me a while ago."

"What could she possibly say that we'd care about?"

"You'd be surprised. Careful now."

Josh slowed at the door and looked through the glass. He saw a stairwell area, with the bearded stranger just starting up the stairs.

"After him," Josh said, pushing the doors open. "But don't make any noise, and stay back so he can't see us."

The carpets muffled the boys' footsteps as they reached the landing, where they turned to climb the last steps to the next deck.

"I don't see him," Josh whispered.

"He can't have just disappeared," Tank answered.

"I know, but I still don't see him." Josh quickly climbed the remaining stairs. There was no one around. From the stairwell, a corridor on the left led to one row of staterooms. Another corridor led to staterooms behind and to the boys' right.

Josh pointed. "You go to the right. I'll take the left. Meet back here in a few minutes. I'm going to get to the bottom of this—if it's the last thing I ever do."

Tank groaned. "That's what scares me!"

Chapter Four

A PLAN TO GET EVEN

At the dinner table, Kanani and Vicki had watched Josh and Tank's sudden departure with great curiosity. Kanani impulsively pushed back her half-eaten strawberry ice cream and asked her mother if she could be excused. Vicki did the same.

As soon as the girls had left the dining room and entered the stairwell area in front of an elevator, Kanani saw that neither Josh nor Tank was in sight.

"Where did they go?" Kanani wondered aloud. "And why did they jump up and leave so fast?"

Vicki glanced around. "I don't know, but I'd sure like to find out. Anyway, I did tell Josh that you had to talk to him because he might be in danger."

Kanani snapped, "You shouldn't have done that!"

"Why not?" Vicki demanded defensively.

"Just because. That's why."

"That's no answer! Anyway, Josh should now be anxious to find you."

Kanani didn't want to give her real reason—that she herself wanted to give Josh the news about somebody hiding something in his bag. Suddenly Kanani saw an opportunity to not explain her motive. She whispered, "Here comes the government agent I told you about."

The short, stocky man with the red hair hurriedly entered from the left-hand double deck doors and approached the elevator where the girls stood.

"Allow me," he said, reaching for the call buttons. "You going up or down?"

"Either way," Vicki said.

"Exploring the ship, are you?" he asked, pushing the *Up* button.

"Sort of," Vicki replied.

"Your first cruise?"

Both girls nodded. Vicki, apparently excited that she was talking to a secret agent, introduced herself and Kanani and told where they were from. The red-haired man didn't volunteer his name or hometown.

Kanani didn't want to get involved in a conversation with this man. She was fearful that Vicki might blurt out something about their knowing who he really was.

"Uh," Kanani said, "my friend and I don't need to wait for the elevator. We can take the stairs. Come on, Vicki."

"No, Kanani, let's wait." Vicki looked up at the red-haired man. "What did you say your name was?"

He smiled and jabbed the elevator button again. "I didn't say. But it's Corby Tilford."

Kanani thought, *I doubt that's his real name.*

Vicki casually asked, "What do you do, Mr. Tilford?"

"I'm a financial investor."

Vicki said with seeming innocence, "You look more like a secret government agent to us."

Kanani was so shocked that she jabbed her elbow into the girl's ribs, but Vicki didn't seem to notice. However, Kanani saw the man's eyes narrow for just a second.

Then he asked, "Why do you think that?"

Before Vicki could explain, Kanani said sharply, "Let's go, Vicki!" She grabbed her new friend's arm and pulled her toward the stairs so fast that the girl almost stumbled.

At the landing, when they were out of the man's sight, Vicki jerked her arm away from Kanani. "Why did you do that?" Vicki demanded hotly. "I've never talked to a secret agent before! Now you've spoiled it."

"No, you've spoiled it!" Kanani flared. "He's going to be suspicious of us. He'll wonder what we know, and that could be dangerous! Don't you realize that?"

"How could that be?" Vicki asked defensively. "He's one of the good guys!"

"Just the same, you shouldn't have said anything!"

"You don't have to bite my head off!"

"I'm just trying to make you . . . oops!" Kanani broke off as the outside doors opened. "Shh!" she whispered. "Here come Josh and Tank."

Vicki's anger quickly ebbed. "Good! Now's your chance to tell Josh about his suitcase."

"Remember our plan," Kanani said, heading toward the boys. "You keep Tank away so I can talk to Josh alone."

As the boys came through the doors, Josh said, "Oh no! Here come the girls. Let's just keep walking."

"Too late. They're waving to us."

Josh sighed. "If we walk away, we'll hurt their feelings, but if Kong sees us talking to his sister . . . "

"Don't remind me!" Tank interrupted.

Josh looked around, grateful that Kong wasn't in sight. "Let's get this over with fast."

They walked toward the girls.

Vicki said sharply, "You boys sure left the table in a hurry a while ago."

Kanani laid a hand on Vicki's arm and gave it a warning squeeze. Kanani asked, "You exploring the ship?"

Tank replied, "You might say that."

"Good!" Vicki exclaimed. "We haven't seen it yet, so why don't you show us around? Come on, Kanani. You walk with Josh while Tank and I go ahead."

"Uh . . . ," Tank began, casting a pleading glance at Josh. "We can't, huh, Josh?"

Josh nodded vigorously. "That's right. We're on our way to do something."

"We'll go with you," Kanani eagerly volunteered.

"You can't!" Tank protested. "Josh, tell them why."

"Me?" Josh asked, startled. When Tank nodded, Josh thought fast, thinking how to avoid telling a lie and yet not daring to say that he was afraid of what Kong might do if he knew Josh and Tank were with Kanani.

Unable to think of a logical excuse, Josh finally said rather lamely, "Just because."

Vicki protested, "But it's important! Josh, you've *got* to walk with her."

Josh's suspicions and annoyance were instantly aroused. He vigorously shook his head. "No, I don't."

A hurt expression spread over Kanani's face. She cried, "I was trying to help you, Josh! That's all! You're in danger, but you won't listen! Well, I've done my best!" She whirled and ran away.

"Wait, Kanani!" Josh called. "I didn't mean . . . "

Vicki interrupted. "You shouldn't have done that, Josh," she said severely. "You'll be sorry! Real sorry!" She hurried after Kanani.

Josh watched them go. "I'm already sorry," he said. "Yeah," Tank agreed. "Me, too. But things will be worse if she tells Kong about this."

Josh turned away with a sigh, then stiffened. "She won't have to. Look who's coming."

Tank took a quick look and sucked in his breath. "Kong! Do you suppose he saw us talking to them?"

Josh thought fast. "No, I don't think so. If he had, he'd be roaring down on us like a runaway train. Hmm . . . I wonder who that is with him?"

"Never mind about him! Let's duck onto the deck, out of the way."

"Hey, haole boys!" Kong called as the boys hurriedly started to exit. "Wait up, yeah?"

Tank groaned. "Too late! Now we're going to get it."

"It wasn't your fault," Josh replied, stopping beside his friend as Kong and the unknown boy approached. "I'll explain . . . "

"You can't explain anything to Kong! You know that!"

"I have to try," Josh said, taking another look at Kong's companion. He was a short, dark-haired boy who could have been part of Hawaii's large Japanese-American population.

"You malihinis," Kong said, approaching and clapping a huge hand on his companion's shoulder. "Dis heah da kine friend Kong meet dis ship, yeah?"

The other boy smiled and nodded. "Kamuela has told me about you two. I'm Micah Kajiwara*."

Josh sighed with relief, realizing that Kong had not seen him and Tank talking to the girls. So Josh introduced himself and Tank to Micah and asked where he was from.

"Near Livingston, California," he replied. "My parents and grandparents own a little farm there in the San Joaquin Valley. I'm traveling with my grand . . . "

"Enough da talk," Kong interrupted. He hurried off.

Micah hung back. "Maybe we could all go swimming in the ship's pool later," he suggested.

Kong stopped, looked back, and shook his massive head. "No swim dose pupule* haoles. Heli mai*, come here, Micah."

Micah waved a little uncertainly to Josh and Tank before following Kong.

Josh watched them go. "Whew! That's a relief."

"Yeah. Now that Kong's met a friend, maybe he'll quit bothering us."

"Micah seems like a nice guy," Josh replied, "but there's not much chance of getting to know him with Kong around."

Josh and Tank had just started walking again when Tank pointed. "Look! There's the bearded man again!"

He was heading away from the boys as Josh exclaimed, "Let's follow him! And this time, we won't lose him!"

* * *

After leaving Josh, Kanani tried to drown her hurt and anger in a cold glass of cola. She and Vicki sat at a table by the open-air snack stand on a deck near the ship's stern*. Kanani was doodling on her paper napkin with a pencil some-one had left behind on the metal table.

"Josh was mean!" Kanani fumed, her fingers moving in short, sure strokes. "I could just die of embarrassment!"

"It wasn't just you," Vicki said consolingly. "Did you see how Tank looked when I suggested he and I walk on ahead? The truth is that they just didn't want to be seen with either of us. They think they're too good for us."

Kanani didn't reply as she switched from idle doodling to sketching on the paper napkin.

Vicki asked, "You know what we should do? Get even with them."

Kanani stopped her drawing and looked across the table at Vicki. "How would we do that?"

"I'll have to think about it. Say, you're really good at draw-ing. In fact, that's very good."

"It's just a quick sketch."

"It's great. Is it okay if I keep it?"

Kanani shrugged and pushed the napkin across the white metal tabletop. "Sure."

"Thanks." Vicki admired the pencil drawing of the ship's deck at night with the lights strung overhead on long wires over the swimming pool. "I guess artistic talent runs in your family, huh? I mean, with your brother winning this trip with his . . . "

"It's nothing!" Kanani interrupted a little sharply. "Forget it."

Vicki shrugged, then her eyes lit up through the glasses. "Hey! I just got an idea. We could snub Josh and Tank and not speak to them the rest of the trip. That'll make them think twice about how they treat us."

"They're already avoiding us. They'd probably be glad if we snubbed them," Kanani replied sourly. She wished that weren't so, because she didn't have many opportunities to make friends. At school, Josh and Tank had always been nice to her, although they kept their distance. Still, she was upset at the way Josh had just treated her.

Vicki carefully folded the napkin drawing. "Hey! I know something that'll work!"

"What's that?"

Vicki's words came out in a rush. "We just won't tell Josh that the bearded man hid something in his suitcase. That way he's on his own, and he deserves whatever happens to him!"

"I don't know . . . "

"Just don't tell him," Vicki interrupted. "Okay?"

Slowly taking a deep breath, Kanani felt her humiliation start to ease off. She said, "The secret agent will probably catch the bearded man anyway, and then Josh wouldn't be in danger."

"Mr. Tilford is obviously more interested in finding whatever was hidden in Josh's bag."

"It does seem that way. The agent probably won't do anything until he knows where whatever he's looking for is hidden. He would most likely wait until he's sure the crook has it again. But how's he going to get into Josh's room and recover the hidden item?"

"He'll find a way," Vicki assured Kanani. "A little thing like that won't stop a crook."

"You're probably right. So when the crook gets this thing back, Josh won't be in any more danger. But what happens if Josh comes in while the crook is recovering the hidden item? He could hurt Josh."

"That's a risk Josh will have to take, because you tried to tell him and he just made you angry."

"Still, I wouldn't want him to be hurt. Or Tank."

"So then it's agreed: we won't tell Josh anything."

Slowly, Kanani nodded. "I guess that's okay."

"Great! Then we'll see what happens when the crook tries to get his stolen stuff back from Josh's suitcase!"

Kanani picked up another napkin and started doodling again. "I just hope nothing unexpected happens that gets us all in trouble."

"Relax! How could anything like that happen?"

Kanani didn't answer, but she felt uneasy. She remembered the way Tilford's eyes had narrowed when Vicki blurted out that she thought he was a secret agent.

He was suspicious, Kanani told herself with assurance, doodling along. Aloud, she explained, "The red-haired man's going to wonder how you guessed what he is. Then he's probably going to start investigating us to find out what else we know. That could get us both in trouble."

"Ahh," Vicki scoffed. "He'll figure we're just a couple of kids playing guessing games."

"Maybe, but what happens if we're wrong about this?" Kanani looked back over the stern at the ship's white wake stretching into the vast, empty ocean.

Then, in spite of the warm, gentle breeze, she shivered.

Chapter Five

THE THREAT

Josh and Tank had no trouble trailing the bearded man when he took the stairs down instead of the elevator. The boys held back until the man reached the fifth deck and turned into the port corridor. They gave him a few seconds start; then they, too, entered the corridor.

It was empty except for a cabin steward with his wheeled supply cart. The boys hurried toward him.

Josh explained, "We're looking for a bearded man who just came down this way. Which is his cabin?"

"Number 5025," the steward replied, pointing. "I'm just about to turn down his bed for the night."

"Thanks," Josh said, satisfied. He turned away and lowered his voice. "Follow my lead, Tank." Josh walked up to number 5025 and lifted his hand as though to knock. Then he stopped and hurried back to the steward.

"Did you say you haven't yet turned down his bed?"

"No. I usually do that while everyone's at dinner, but he had a *Do Not Disturb* sign on until just a minute ago when he returned. He must have forgotten to remove it before he went out earlier."

42

"Then we'd better not interfere with your work," Josh replied. "Besides, he is probably anxious to get to bed. Come on, Tank. We can see him tomorrow."

As the boys hurriedly walked away, Tank grinned. "Good thinking, Josh! For a second there, you scared me when I thought you were really going to knock. I couldn't think what you might say to him if he opened the door."

Josh grinned. "Neither could I. Anyway, now let's find the purser's desk. We'll get the passenger list and find the name of our mysterious bearded man."

The boys returned to the elevator and stairwell area to consult a diagram of the ship posted on the wall under glass. The purser's counter was shown to be in the middle of the ship and one deck down, by the activities desk.

The boys rushed down the stairs. Josh was disappointed to see that there were several people standing in line in front of the purser's counter, waiting for service. At the head of the line, a heavyset woman was chattering away at the uniformed girl behind the counter as she cashed a hundred-dollar traveler's check.

Across the wide corridor, passengers at the activities desk were picking up free papers that listed scheduled programs or information on buying shore-excursion tickets. Mr. Ladd had already purchased tickets for his party.

Josh lowered his voice so the other people in line ahead and behind could not hear. "Tank, I keep thinking of what Vicki said about Kanani wanting to talk to me. I'm really sorry that she misunderstood me."

"It doesn't matter. She's still mad."

"Yes, but I've got to find a way to ask Kanani what she knows that made Vicki tell me I was in trouble."

"Oh, sure!" Tank said softly, a tinge of sarcasm in his tone. "That's easy! You just have to get her to speak to you, which she won't. Then, if you even try to talk to her and Kong sees you, he'll pound you flat."

The heavyset woman finally walked away from the purser's counter. Two middle-aged women were next. Josh heard them say that they each wanted to break fifty-dollar bills into smaller denominations.

"I wish they'd hurry with this line," Josh said under his breath. "Ordinarily, I wouldn't care. But we need that passenger list fast. When we know who the bearded man is, maybe we can begin to make sense of all the strange things that have been going on."

"Yeah. I can't see how Kanani would know any more than we do," Tank said.

"It all goes back to the terminal when those two men came rushing in late. There was something suspicious about them. Then that bearded man told our cabin steward that he was my father, so Erek unlocked our room and let him in. But why did the man want to get in there?"

Tank shrugged. "Don't ask me."

Josh continued thoughtfully, "It must have some connection with what Vicki meant when she said Kanani thinks I'm in trouble because of something I have. But I don't have anything."

"Kanani thinks you do, but she won't tell you now."

"If I'm in danger, I need to know why, so she's *got* to tell me."

Josh fell silent as an elderly, baldish man moved to the purser's counter and said he had lost his boarding pass. He understood that it would be needed to return to the ship after going ashore at Puerto Vallarta*. The assistant purser confirmed this and issued a new card.

At last it was Josh's turn at the counter. He said, "I'd like a list of all the passengers, please."

"Sorry, but you're at the wrong counter." The assistant purser pointed across the corridor. "You'll find that at the activities desk."

Josh suppressed a groan and managed to say, "Thanks," before turning away. He was relieved to see a small sign: *Passenger List. Take One.*

He hurriedly picked up a list and glanced at it. "I should have guessed this would happen," he exclaimed disgustedly. "All names are in alphabetical order, with their cabin numbers following. We'll have to do this the hard way."

Josh led the way around the people lined up at the activities counter. He plopped down on a large sofa against the far wall and used his fingernail to remove the staple from the passenger list.

"Here," he said, handing half the sheets to Tank. "You start looking for Cabin 5025. I'll do the same with these pages."

Tank took the sheets and turned to the last page.

"There are 805 passengers listed! This will take hours."

"Then let's get started," Josh answered. He ran his finger

down the page, ignoring the names to focus exclusively on the stateroom numbers.

After several minutes, he finished his sheets and turned to Tank. "I didn't see it."

"I'm almost through, and nothing so far."

Josh realized it was possible that the bearded man in Cabin 5025 might have not booked passage in time to have his name printed. Josh shook off that thought and glanced hopefully at Tank.

"I'm almost to the Z's," he said softly, eyes still on the sheet. "Just a few more . . . wait!" He bent closer to the sheet. "Yes, here it is! Number 5025. Baxter Yount."

"Let me see!" Josh exclaimed, leaning close to where Tank's finger rested. "Baxter Yount," Josh repeated softly. "Now we have a name for the bearded man."

"But we still don't know how this ties in with what Kanani knows," Tank said.

"We've got to find out." Josh glanced at the brass-encased clock on the wall. "It's pretty late, but let's go see if we can find those girls before bedtime."

He folded the passenger list sheets, shoved them in his back pants pocket, and stood up.

Tank protested, "You're trying your best to have Kong beat us up, aren't you?"

"You don't have to come," Josh said.

"I know, but maybe Kong won't see us, and I do want to be there to see how you get Kanani to talk to you."

"I'll start by apologizing. Then I hope they'll listen. Well, are you coming?"

Tank took a long, slow breath and noisily blew it out before answering. "What kind of a friend would I be if I let you risk running into Kong alone?"

The boys hurried away from the purser's area toward the elevator. Josh was having second thoughts about Tank.

He's willing to come along with me because we're friends, but what kind of a friend am I if I get him hurt in a situation that I should handle by myself? I'd better not take that chance.

Thinking fast, Josh stopped in front of the elevator and pushed the call button. He made up his mind. He told himself, *I have got to find Kanani, but I don't want to risk Tank getting hurt if I also run into Kong.*

He said to Tank, "I should have my video camera to shoot some footage of the ship at night under the lights."

"Then, let's go get it."

"We'd lose too much time. Look, why don't you get it while I look for the girls?"

"What if you run into Kong?"

"I'll be careful. I'll go onto the top deck and work my way down. You find the camera and do the same. Let's meet back at our cabin in half an hour. Okay?"

Tank shrugged and got off at the seventh deck. Josh rode up to the top deck, where there was a shuffleboard area at the ship's stern. Josh thought this was as good as any place to start looking for Kanani.

* * *

Kanani had already returned to her family's stateroom. The sound of running water came faintly from the tiny bathroom where Mrs. Kong was taking a shower. Kanani climbed into the top bunk, which had been lowered into place for the night. She dangled her feet over the side and stared unseeingly at her hands. Her brother watched her suspiciously from his bed below, which had been turned down for sleeping.

Kong asked, "Why foh you look like dat, huh?"

Slowly, his little sister roused herself from deep thought and looked at him. "What?"

Kong's brown eyes narrowed. "You t'ink maybe so tell 'bout da picture, yeah?"

For a second, Kanani didn't understand. When she did, she shook her head. "No, no. I told you I wouldn't do that, and I won't."

Her giant of a brother started to smile, then stopped, cocking his head to look at her again. "Den why foh you got long face, huh?"

Kanani felt guilty about keeping her secret from Josh, but she couldn't tell her brother that. She jumped down from the upper bed. "It's none of your business, Kamuela!" She crossed quickly to the door.

"Where you go, huh?" he demanded.

"That's none of your business, either!" She pulled the door open and stepped into the deserted corridor. As the door closed behind her, she hesitated.

What should I do? she asked herself. *If I don't tell Josh what I know, that crook might do something awful to him, especially if Josh is there when the thief tries to get into Josh's bag.*

Kanani's first inclination was to approach Vicki's cabin and see if she was still awake. Then Kanani shook her head. *I'd better just take a walk by myself and think about this,* she decided, and headed down the long corridor.

At the stairwell she pushed open the heavy side doors and stepped onto the well-lighted starboard*-side promenade deck. It was silent and totally deserted.

The breezes, coming off the bow, weren't quite as warm as the familiar Hawaiian trade winds, but they were still very pleasant on her cheeks.

She walked a few steps toward the bow to get away from the bright lights by the door. Where the light fell away, she leaned against the polished wooden rail and looked across the ocean, deep in thought.

She had never seen such darkness. Earlier the captain had announced that they were cruising ten nautical miles offshore, yet there was no sign of land, no lights from homes or fishing boats—nothing but total blackness. She didn't know if they were already off the coast of the Baja peninsula*, but thought that was possible.

The sky, filled with a myriad of tiny stars, should have been glorious to her, but it wasn't. Instead, it was a vast darkness threatening to descend on her. Her mood matched that darkness.

Kanani let her gaze drift down. The only exception to the blackness of the night was a curl of white foam thrown back by the ship's bow. The incessant waves hissed menacingly as they vanished into the dark.

Kanani warned herself, *If something happens to Josh, it'll be my fault. But he made me so mad the way he treated me! I'm so mixed up that I don't know what to do!*

She interrupted her thinking at the sound of someone starting to open the starboard-side doors leading from the deck. She glanced back.

It's Josh! Now's my chance, she told herself, then shook her head. *I can't do it—not yet, anyway.*

She silently hurried away toward the ship's bow. There she could see that the deck narrowed to about four feet wide where part of the ship's superstructure stuck out. She looked back just as Josh started toward her.

I don't think he saw me, she told herself, moving quietly into an area about thirty feet long where there were no lights.

The breeze, forced through the narrow opening between the superstructure and the railing, was suddenly so strong that Kanani was almost thrown off balance. She leaned forward and lowered her eyes to watch the deck. It was now barely visible by the faint light that filtered in from bulbs behind and at the bow some forty feet ahead. She glanced back.

Josh was still walking toward her, looking seaward. Behind him, Kanani saw the double doors open and the bearded man step onto the deck. But Josh didn't notice.

It's him! Kanani realized. *He's following Josh, and there's nobody else out here except him and me! But he doesn't know I'm here, and Josh doesn't either.*

Kanani's heart began thudding against her ribs. She

glanced about, hoping to see someone strolling along the deck, but there was nobody. She looked up at the next deck where the 60-passenger lifeboats were suspended, hopefully never to be needed.

I know! Kanani thought. *I can run around the front and climb to the deck on the other side. Then I'll come back through the stairwell area and out the door on this side. I can look down from that deck and see what happens on this one. If I can get there in time, I can shout to warn Josh if the man tries to hurt him.*

* * *

Josh suddenly stopped, peering into the darkened area by the superstructure. He had caught a glimpse of someone running out of the darkness and into the bright lights of the bow. The fleeing figure was gone in a second, but Josh was almost sure he had seen Kanani.

She's running away from me, he told himself, *but I've got to talk to her.* He broke into a run, unaware that there was anyone behind him.

In the dark, narrow space between the superstructure and rail, the unexpected powerful gust of wind made him stagger. He caught his balance and ran on. He burst into the full glare of the lights on the bow deck and stopped.

She's gone. Josh glanced around, but saw only the empty deck and the machinery on the very front of the steel bow one deck down. The ship's bow rose and fell slowly as it plowed through the darkness.

With a resigned sigh, Josh turned back, knowing there was

no way of guessing where Kanani had gone to elude him. He slowly left the lighted bow deck area and reentered the narrow, dark space between the superstructure and rail.

His eyes had not adjusted from the change of lighted bow deck to darkness, so he collided with someone.

"Oops! Sorry!" Josh exclaimed. "I didn't see you."

"No harm done," a man's voice replied. He added quickly, "Beautiful night, isn't it?"

In the pale reflected light, Josh could barely make out that the stranger was tall and slender. His face was indistinct. "Yes, it is." Josh leaned against the rail beside him. "Without a moon, those stars are just little specks, and they look so far away."

The stranger leaned over the rail and looked down where the ship's bow was plowing the sea back into hissing white curls.

"If somebody fell overboard at night," he said softly, "with no one around, he'd never be found."

There was something about the man's tone that made Josh glance sharply at him, but Josh was distracted by a sudden sharp intake of breath above him. He looked up at the next deck, but couldn't see anybody.

"Thought I heard somebody up there," he said, turning back toward the man.

He was gone. He had moved away on catlike feet, heading aft on the promenade deck.

Josh watched the man's slender body as he stepped into the light. There he stopped and glanced back.

Josh sucked in his breath. "It's him!" he exclaimed softly

into the night. "Baxter Yount, the bearded man in Cabin 5025."

He added silently, *I think he just threatened me!*

Chapter Six

THE MYSTERY DEEPENS

Anxious to tell Tank about the strange encounter with the bearded passenger, Baxter Yount, Josh ran back to the Ladds' stateroom. There he reached for his key.

That's strange, he told himself, carefully checking his pockets. *How could I have lost it?*

He quickly retraced his steps, eyes scanning the carpeted corridor as he passed the line of inside and outside cabins. He searched the promenade deck back to the dark, windy corner, where he knelt and swept his hands back and forth in the darkness. He did not find the key and returned to knock at his stateroom door.

Tank opened it. "Why didn't you use your key?"

Josh saw that Erek had turned down the two beds and lowered the upper one so all were ready for the night. Mr. Ladd looked up from where he was sitting on his bed and typing on his portable computer.

Josh started to explain about the key, but Tank interrupted. "Guess who was here a minute ago?" Without waiting for Josh to reply, Tank added, "Kanani!"

Josh instantly forgot about the missing key. "I looked all over for her. What did she want?"

Tank shrugged. "She wouldn't say."

Mr. Ladd asked, "Son, what's going on?"

Josh hesitated, glancing at Tank, who shrugged but said nothing. Josh looked back at his father and then briefly told him everything. He began with the suspicious actions of the two men in the terminal and ended with the ominous words moments ago by the bearded man.

Josh concluded, "It wasn't really a direct threat, Dad. Mr. Yount might have just been making a comment."

"We can't take any chances," Mr. Ladd said, looking at his wristwatch. "It's too late to call the Kongs' cabin tonight. But first thing in the morning, I'd like to talk with Mrs. Kong and those girls about all this."

"Oh, Dad," Josh protested, "do we have to do that? I mean, Tank and I could . . . "

His father interrupted. "I suspect it's not nearly as serious as you seem to think, but I'm not going to take any chances. Now, let's all get some sleep."

* * *

Josh lay in his narrow bed, thinking. He felt the gentle rise and fall of the ship as it sliced through calm seas. He heard the faint squeak of hidden timbers inside the walls. He knew that he had done the right thing in telling his father, yet regretted that he had not been able to solve this mystery on his own.

Then Josh sighed. *But this one is hard, and I don't even*

know when or how I lost my key. It's probably a good thing that Dad's going to talk to Mrs. Kong. He closed his eyes and drifted off to sleep.

He awakened to see faint light seeping through the shades drawn over the outside window. Josh could hear Tank's gentle snoring. Mr. Ladd's top sheet had been thrown back, showing that he had left his bed. This didn't surprise Josh because his dad was always an early riser. Josh guessed that his father had quietly dressed and left the stateroom, probably in search of a cup of coffee.

Josh sat up and swung his feet over the side of the bed, feeling for his slippers with his toes. He reached for the small flashlight that he always placed near the head of a bed when he was in a hotel room or other strange place. Josh put his fingers across the lens and snapped on the light. He allowed only a small shaft of light to escape between his fingers so he could see to walk, but not enough to disturb Tank. Josh moved silently toward the bathroom.

As he passed the open closet, he saw that his bag had somehow fallen forward so it lay partially on the cabin floor. Josh lifted the empty bag by one corner and gently placed it farther back in the closet.

He started toward the cabin door, then stopped, frowning. He had felt something through the bag's fabric that he didn't remember feeling before. He turned back to the closet and spread his fingers slightly, permitting extra light to show on the bag.

He ran his free hand over the outside of the bag and traced the outline of a small, barely discernible object that wasn't quite square. He quietly unzipped the bag, allowing the thin beam of light to reveal a small raised area inside the top lining.

Hmm? What's that? He could see the outline of a flat object about four inches long, almost square, and about the thickness of a wire coat hanger. Josh saw where the lining had been cut and then sealed. Using a fingernail to reopen the cut, he carefully reached inside the lining and lifted out something that looked familiar.

In doing so, he dropped the flashlight, awakening Tank, who demanded sleepily, "What are you doing?"

"Look what I found," Josh replied. He reached over to the wall switch and turned on the cabin light.

"Hey!" Tank grumbled, covering his eyes with his hands. "You trying to blind me?"

Josh ignored the remark. "Take a look at this."

Tank lowered his hands, blinked a couple of times, then looked at the object extended toward him. "It's just one of your dad's disks that he uses in his portable computer. Why did you wake me up for this?"

"It's not Dad's," Josh explained, tapping the small silvery label that read *Micro Floppy Disk*. "Dad always puts an identifying label on his disks. Besides, he wouldn't have hidden it in my bag." Josh showed Tank where he had found the disk.

"Then, how did it get there?" Tank wanted to know.

Josh replied thoughtfully, "I think that either the bearded man or the redheaded man must have done it while the bags were waiting to be loaded onto the ship. Or maybe after it came aboard, but before it was delivered to our cabin."

"Why would either of them do that?"

"Probably because whoever it was had to hide it in a hurry, and my bag was handy."

Tank reached out, took the disk, and carefully looked it over. "It must have something very valuable on it to make someone do that."

"That's my guess, too."

"But," Tank mused, returning the disk to Josh, "if that's so, whoever put it there will want it back."

Josh's eyes widened in understanding. "Of course! Like the bearded man . . . "

"Yount," Tank broke in. "Baxter Yount."

Josh nodded and continued, "He told the steward he was my dad so that Erek would unlock the cabin door and let him in so he could recover this!"

"Yeah! That makes sense. He must have been frightened away before he had time to find the disk. That means he still has to try getting it back. But how will he get in? Erek won't let . . . "

Josh interrupted. "With my key! I didn't lose it! Yount must have taken it from me last night when we bumped into each other in the darkness on deck!"

"I think you're right," Tank agreed. "Hey, maybe Kanani knows something about this, and that's why she wants to see you right away this . . . !"

Josh held up his hand, breaking into Tank's sentence. "Wait! Wait! I just thought of something else! Now that Yount has my key, he'll need to try to get this disk back the first chance he has."

"Like when we go to the Kongs' cabin or to breakfast! How are we going to keep him from getting it?"

Josh considered that question. "We can either hide it someplace else or take it with us," Josh mused. "But first, I'd sure like to know what's on this thing."

"There's an easy way to find out," Tank replied. "Open your father's portable computer and . . . "

"Wait a minute! You know how careful Dad is with his computer. He won't let me touch it unless he's right there watching me."

Tank glanced at Mr. Ladd's empty bed and then the open bathroom door. "Where is he?"

"Probably having a cup of coffee, but the dining room isn't open yet, and I don't know where else he could find coffee this early in the morning. Let's get dressed and go find him."

When the boys opened their stateroom door, Erek was just starting down the far end of the corridor pushing his cart loaded with cabin supplies.

Josh and Tank asked the room steward where coffee was being served now. Erek replied that an early-bird breakfast was served at 6:30 each morning on the stern of the eighth deck.

Josh and Tank thanked Erek and hurried away. Josh commented that Yount, the bearded man, wouldn't dare risk using Josh's key while the steward was around.

The boys found Mr. Ladd sipping coffee and getting acquainted with a half-dozen other early risers seated at small round metal tables in the brisk morning air.

The boys motioned for him to join them, so he carried his cup to where they impatiently waited by the stern rail. Behind them, the ship's wake made a wide silvery pattern that stretched out about a half-mile on the calm seas.

"What are you boys so excited about?" Mr. Ladd asked.

Josh showed the disk and told how he had found it and guessed that the disk contained valuable information. He added that he thought his missing key probably would be used to try recovering the disk.

When Josh had finished his explanation, Mr. Ladd set his cup on an empty table and started across the deck. "Come on," he said. "Let's get my computer and see what we're dealing with. Then maybe I'll call security and let them handle it."

"Aw, Dad!" Josh protested as he followed his father's long-legged stride into the ship's interior. "That's going to take all the fun out of it! Tank and I want to solve this case ourselves."

"It might be dangerous, son. Besides, that's why ships have security personnel."

Josh was keenly disappointed, but he also recognized the wisdom of his father's decision.

In the stateroom, Mr. Ladd turned on his computer and inserted the disk Josh had found. Tank joined them in leaning forward to see what came up on the screen. There was only one item listed on the menu: Apex-One.

Mr. Ladd said, "I'll bring that file up on the screen and see what Apex-One is." His fingers moved on the keys, causing the menu to vanish and be replaced by a large intricate drawing.

Tank sighed in disappointment. "It's nothing but a bunch of

lines, like a blueprint."

"It's a schematic," Mr. Ladd explained. "A diagram or plan of something technical. See the way the wiring is depicted?"

"Whatever it is," Tank commented, turning away unhappily, "it doesn't look valuable to me."

Josh asked, "But if it's not valuable, then why did that man go to all the trouble of hiding this disk and then trying to get it back by lying to Erek and stealing my key?"

Mr. Ladd studied the schematic carefully before answering. "I think it is valuable and that you boys have stumbled onto what's called industrial espionage."

Tank's interest returned. "What's that?"

"Industrial espionage has to do with companies spying on each other and trying to steal secrets from another's business, especially in manufacturing," Mr. Ladd explained, still examining the computer screen.

"You mean," Josh asked, "somebody created the plans for this Apex-One thing, whatever it is, and they were stolen?"

"Looks that way," his father replied. "From what little I can understand from this schematic, it seems like an idea for a new electronic system. This disk with the plans was probably being sent to Mexico, where lots of American companies are now relocating. Some items can be manufactured there much cheaper than at home."

"Only it was stolen by this Mr. Yount," Josh finished breathlessly. "Tank, remember when we saw that bearded man acting suspiciously in the terminal building?"

"Yeah! And the redheaded man came in. I'll bet he's a

security man for the company where it was stolen, and he has to get this disk back. Maybe he was about to grab the thief, and so the crook hid the disk in the first place he could find—your suitcase."

"Now, boys," Mr. Ladd cautioned, "this is all supposition. We could be dead wrong about everything—well, except for this." He pointed to the screen. "My guess is that it's a highly secret electronic invention of some sort, and it's certainly important enough that one man is trying to keep it from another. That makes it a matter for the ship's security people." He reached for the telephone.

A few minutes later, a wiry man in a khaki uniform with black shoulder boards* arrived at the cabin. He carried a radio handset and introduced himself as Dave Stark, head of ship security.

He listened while Mr. Ladd showed the schematic on the computer's screen and explained the situation.

When that was done, Stark commented, "I'll look into this right away."

Josh said, "While we were waiting for you, we decided that the bearded man, Yount, will have to try getting that disk back soon so he can pass it on to somebody at our ports of call."

Mr. Ladd added, "Our schedule calls for us to dock Wednesday at Puerto Vallarta, then later at Zihuatenejo*, and finally Acapulco*."

As Stark nodded, Josh asked him, "Why don't you just tell the red-haired man that we have the disk and let him handle the thief?"

"Because," the security chief replied, "we're assuming that everything we've discussed is true, but suppose we're wrong?" He shook his head. "In my work, we don't dare assume anything. I'll quietly do some background investigation on both those men. In the meantime, all of you must promise not to tell anybody about this disk or our conversation. Agreed?"

Josh, his father, and Tank nodded. Then Mr. Ladd said thoughtfully, "Mr. Stark, it makes sense to try having this resolved off the ship so the boys aren't in any danger. But how do you propose to do that?"

"We don't want to make the suspect suspicious, so we have to move carefully. Mr. Ladd, do you have any spare disks like this one the boys found?"

"Yes. Why?"

"Good! We'll use one to set a trap."

"I see," Mr. Ladd replied. "The thief uses Josh's stolen key to recover the disk but gets the wrong one."

"Exactly," Stark agreed. "There will be no reason for him to suspect it's not the same one he hid. Let's hope he doesn't have some way to view it. I'll arrange it so that when he goes ashore and tries to pass on the stolen disk, local authorities will move in. Now, let's get started."

By the time the breakfast chimes sounded, the trap had been set. Josh and Tank followed Mr. Ladd and the security officer from the cabin.

Josh remembered the bearded man's ominous words on the dark deck last night. Would he try to recover the disk while everyone was at breakfast? And why did Kanani want to see Josh as soon as possible?

Whatever it was, he had an uneasy feeling about it.

Chapter Seven

THE TROUBLE WITH SECRETS

As Josh and Tank entered the ship's dining room, Mr. Ladd reminded them that breakfast had open seating. They could sit anywhere they wanted, or even go on deck for cafeteria-style serving. Josh glanced around quickly and saw Mrs. Kong, Mrs. Fyfe, and Kong, but not his new friend Micah Kajiwara, Kanani, or Vicki.

Josh guessed that Micah might have slept in, but that the girls would be at the buffet breakfast. Josh and Tank decided to also eat outside on the open deck. There Josh hoped to find out why Kanani had been looking for him the night before.

"What do you suppose she knows about all this?" he asked Tank, who shrugged. Josh added, "We can't tell her about finding the disk, because Mr. Stark asked us not to, but we can ask Kanani some questions."

The boys found Kanani and Vicki on the sixth deck by the swimming pool. The girls already had their food and were seated at one of the starboard-rail tables.

Josh whispered to Tank, "Try to get Vicki to go with you so I can talk to Kanani alone."

65

The boys approached the girls' table, where Vicki, apparently already coached by Kanani, quickly stood up.

"I forgot to get orange juice," she said. "Tank, would you talk with me while I get it?"

As Tank and Vicki moved away, Kanani motioned for Josh to sit opposite her. He did so, noticing that she had sketched something on a napkin.

"That's very good," he said. "May I see it?"

The girl shrugged, so Josh pulled the drawing to him. It depicted the swimming pool and some passengers standing in the breakfast buffet line, plates in hand.

"I wish I could draw like that," Josh commented. "I think that you could have entered the contest and won instead of your brother."

A red flush tinted her cheeks, and she lowered her eyes. "I got to come anyway."

"That's true," Josh agreed.

Kanani reached across and crumpled the napkin with the drawing on it. Abruptly, she said, "I think you're in danger."

"Oh?"

Kanani glanced around as other passengers walked by with their trays of food. "Yes," she said softly, leaning across the table toward him. "Have you seen a man with a black beard?"

"Yes. His name is Baxter Yount."

Kanani's eyes opened wide. "You know him?"

"No, but I learned that's his name. Do you think I'm in danger from him?"

"Yes, I do."

"Why?"

Kanani briefly told about seeing the bearded man hide something in Josh's bag, then run away just before the red-haired man came along.

"Later," Kanani explained, "Vicki asked the redheaded man his name. He said it was Corby Tilford."

Josh repeated the name. "Corby Tilford." At last he had identification for the second mysterious man on board.

Kanani said, "Vicki started asking him questions. I wish she hadn't done that."

Josh asked sharply, "You told Vicki about this?"

"Yes, but she promised to keep it a secret."

Josh remembered something his father always said: *How can you expect someone to keep a secret when you couldn't keep it secret yourself?*

He wanted to tell Kanani that he had found the disk, but couldn't because of his promise.

Kanani continued, "One more thing: last night I was on the lifeboat deck looking down on that dark part of the deck where you and that bearded man, Baxter Yount, were. I heard him threaten you about going overboard and that nobody would ever find you."

"Maybe it wasn't a threat against me. Maybe he was just making small talk."

Kanani shook her head. "I don't think so. You see, he has to get back whatever it was he hid in your bag. If he doesn't, he'll blame you and . . . " She left her sentence unfinished but looked meaningfully toward the vast, empty Pacific sliding past their ship.

"Thanks for telling me," Josh said. He felt guilty because he could not tell her that the security officer now had the item Yount had hidden in Josh's bag.

"You don't seem very concerned," Kanani said a little stiffly.

"I just don't think there's any danger, that's why."

"You'll feel differently if that bearded man goes to get whatever he hid in your bag and it's not there." Kanani's voice rose slightly. "So you'd better leave it alone. In fact, maybe you should put that bag where he can get to it easily. Then you should be safe."

Josh realized that Kanani was trying to help him, but he also knew things that she didn't, and he couldn't tell her. Maybe Baxter Yount had already used Josh's stolen key to enter the stateroom and recover the disk. Josh hoped that Yount wouldn't find out that Dave Stark had substituted one of Mr. Ladd's disks for the original.

"Thanks, Kanani," he said. "I'll be careful."

She said sharply, "What you really mean is that you don't believe me."

"I believe you, but . . . "

"No, you don't!" She leaped up, knocking her knife to the deck. "If you did, you'd act differently!"

"No, really, Kanani . . . "

"Well, Josh Ladd," she interrupted, "don't say I didn't try to warn you!" She turned and ran toward the doors leading inside the ship, rushing by Tank and Vicki, who were just leaving the buffet area.

Vicki handed her glass of orange juice to Tank. "Set this on the table for me, please," she said hurriedly. "I have to go after her."

* * *

Vicki caught up with Kanani inside the heavy double doors leading to the ship's interior. "What's the matter?" Vicki asked.

"Josh said he believed me, but he didn't act like it! Oh, Vicki, he must think I'm a complete fool!" Tears sprang to Kanani's eyes. "He makes me so mad!"

Vicki asked suspiciously, "Is that all?"

"Yes, of course! What else would it be?"

Vicki cocked her head slightly and looked at her friend with discerning eyes. "You like him, don't you?"

"Who, Josh? Don't make me laugh!"

"You ever liked a boy before?"

"No, and I don't now—especially Josh!"

"He is kind of cute, don't you think?"

"I didn't notice!" Kanani exclaimed before bursting into tears.

Vicki steered Kanani to the nearest chairs, where they sat down. Kanani threw her arms around Vicki and sobbed brokenly. Just then Kong came clumping along in his new tennis shoes, making both girls jump nervously. Kanani turned her face away as Vicki quickly got to her feet and stepped protectively in front of her friend.

Kong complained, "All wahine talk at da table! Kong eat on deck wit' . . . " He broke off and bent to one side, trying to see around Vicki. "Hey, sistah! Why you cry?"

"It's nothing," Vicki said hastily, standing her ground. "Just girl stuff."

Kong ignored Vicki and looked directly at his sister. "Who make you cry, Kanani? I break da face him!"

"No!" Kanani leaped up, hurriedly wiping her eyes with her hand. "Josh didn't mean . . . oh!" she broke off, realizing what she had done.

"Josh be planty* sorry!" Kong said angrily, clenching his massive fists. "Where he, huh?"

"No, Kamuela, please!" Kanani pleaded. "It isn't his fault!"

Kong looked toward the glass doors leading to the deck. Josh and Tank could be seen sitting at a table. Kong headed toward the doors. "I find da kine haole!"

"Wait, Kamuela!" Kanani's voice rose pleadingly, but her brother kept striding purposefully along. She added a warning. "I'll tell Mama!"

The big boy stopped. His mother was the one person he feared. His thoughts were slow, but a fragment of an idea sprang to his mind. He would wait until everyone went ashore at the first port of call. There he would find Josh alone, and then . . . Kong smiled in anticipation.

* * *

After Kanani stormed off, Tank asked what happened. Josh told him while Tank absently drank the glass of orange juice he had carried to the table for Vicki.

Josh concluded, "If I could just tell her that I found the disk and that Mr. Stark has it, then she would understand why I'm not concerned."

"You tried, so forget it." Tank finished the orange juice and set the glass on the tray of a passing busboy. "Instead, let's think about this redheaded man. What did she say his name is?"

"Corby Tilford. Kanani and Vicki think he's a secret agent trying to recover the disk from Mr. Yount, only they don't know it's a disk."

"What do you think?"

"I think we'd better ask the security officer."

"Good idea." Tank stood up. "Let's go find him."

"Not until after we check our stateroom," Josh replied, pushing back his chair. "Let's see if Mr. Yount used my stolen key to recover that disk." Josh headed for the doors to the ship's interior.

The room steward called to the boys as they passed an open stateroom where he was making up the bed. Erek hurried into the corridor, extending a key.

"Did one of you drop this?" he asked, holding the key so the stateroom number showed. "I found it just outside your door a few minutes ago."

"It's mine," Josh admitted. "Thanks, Erek."

Josh and Tank exchanged knowing glances as they hurried to their stateroom. Josh inserted the key, shoved the door open, went directly to the open closet, and picked up his bag.

"The disk is gone," he exclaimed. "See?"

Tank nodded, feeling the place where the disk had been. The cut section flopped down, showing there was nothing behind it.

"The bait has been taken," Josh said, eyes bright with

excitement. He headed for the door. "Let's go tell Dad—and then Mr. Stark."

Josh and Tank found Mr. Ladd lingering over coffee at the dining room table and talking with Mrs. Kong and Mrs. Fyfe. The boys didn't approach the table, but motioned to Mr. Ladd. He excused himself and hurried toward them.

"Dad, I got my key back," Josh said with suppressed excitement. "But the disk is gone!"

"Good!" Mr. Ladd nodded with satisfaction. "Let's hope Baxter Yount doesn't have a computer. If he does, and he plays that disk and finds out it's a substitute . . . "

"Don't say it, Dad!" Josh exclaimed, trying not to think what the bearded man might do to him.

Mr. Ladd nodded. "Let's go back to our cabin and phone for Dave Stark, the security officer. It'll be easier for him to come to us than to try finding him."

Within a few minutes, Stark arrived at the Ladds' cabin. He examined the bag while the boys explained the latest developments.

Josh finished by asking, "What do you think will happen now, Mr. Stark?"

"It's logical that this Yount fellow will try to pass the disk on to a contact in Mexico. There's a problem in that because we don't know in which port of call that's to be done."

"What about the redheaded man?" Josh asked. He briefly repeated what he had seen in the terminal and what Kanani had told him about Corby Tilford.

"I did some checking on him," the security chief replied.

"If he's who we think he is, he's in some kind of investments."

"But," Josh protested, "would an investment man have followed Baxter Yount as Kanani says he did?"

The officer shrugged. "I don't know yet, but I'll continue my investigation. Meanwhile, we maintain strict silence about this. We make our first stop tomorrow at Puerto Vallarta, so I'll notify local authorities by radio. They can follow either or both suspects. Let's hope we can wrap up this whole thing without anyone except us knowing what's happened."

Josh and Tank spent the rest of the day staying out of Kong's way and thinking about what would happen if the bearded man found out his disk had been switched.

"If that happens," Tank said gloomily, "he'll know that you must have found his original disk. He'll come looking for you."

"Yes, but Yount might also think that somehow the red-headed man, Tilford, had found it."

"How could he do that?" Tank asked scornfully. "From what Kanani told you, Tilford has no idea that the bearded man hid the disk in your bag."

Josh reluctantly admitted, "You're right. If Mr. Yount finds out that his disk has been switched with one of Dad's, he'll figure I have the original. He'd naturally try to get it back. If he got me alone, and I told him that the security officer has the original disk, then maybe . . . "

Josh left his terrible thought unspoken, but Tank finished it for him. "Maybe he meant what he said about somebody going overboard and never being found."

"Both of us have to be careful," Josh warned. "We're

together all the time. If Yount finds out about the switched disks, he'll think you're in on it, too."

Tank groaned and slapped his open palm against his forehead. "I never thought of that! Boy, sometimes I wish I had another best friend who didn't get me in trouble all the time!"

"We're not in trouble yet."

"Maybe not from those two men, but you can't forget about Kong. If he finds out you made his little sister cry . . . "

"I know!" Josh interrupted. "Someday I'm going to have to face him. Maybe if I can get him to talk for a minute before he starts pounding on me, I can figure out what makes him hate me so much."

Tank shook his head. "Don't try to face him. Just run. Otherwise, he'll have you punched out before you can even start talking to him."

"I can't run forever, Tank. Sooner or later, I've got to face him and try to resolve this."

"You can't reason with hatred. But if Kong catches you alone on shore, I wouldn't count on him talking before he clobbers you. So you'd better stick close to your dad because Kong would tackle both you and me and probably beat up on both of us."

"I can't hang around my father like a little kid," Josh replied thoughtfully. He added, "I've prayed for Kong so often, because we're supposed to pray for our enemies. But so far, nothing's changed."

"Just don't let him get you alone," Tank warned.

"That's not going to be easy," Josh said somberly, "because

you and I should split up tomorrow."

"What?" Tank's voice almost cracked.

Josh nodded. "That way, we could each follow one of those men. Maybe you take the redheaded one and I'll follow the bearded . . . "

"No way!" Tank interrupted vehemently. "Not me!"

Josh started to reply, but the ship's public-address system interrupted. "In preparation for your first shore excursion tomorrow," the woman's voice said, "a free lecture will be held in fifteen minutes in the ship's lounge. Instruction will be given in basic Spanish, along with some shopping tips and other pertinent information."

"Come on," Josh said, anxious to change the subject. "We should hear this."

The boys attended, picking up a few Spanish words, but Josh's mind dwelled mostly on tomorrow.

He told himself, *It's going to be an exciting day, and maybe a dangerous one.*

Chapter Eight

WHAT MAKES KONG SO MEAN?

On Wednesday, the ship reached Puerto Vallarta, Mexico, about 1,112 nautical miles from Los Angeles. Another ship was already docked at the wharf, forcing the *Far Horizons* to drop anchor in the bay.

Kanani was excited about going ashore for the first time and about an idea that had come to her during the night.

She shared her thoughts with Vicki, who said, "It might be dangerous, but let's do it!"

"Okay, but we'll have to watch for a time to see Mr. Tilford alone," Kanani replied. "Maybe we can do that if he goes ashore today."

The public-address system announced that while local Mexican authorities were clearing the ship for passengers to land, all those wanting to go ashore were to assemble in the sixth-deck lounge.

Disembarkation would be according to different colored tickets. When someone on the public-address system called a color, all those holding a matching color ticket were to make their way down to the third deck. There, at the waterline, they would board orange-colored boats called tenders for the trip from the ship to the shore. Passengers could then explore on their own by taxi or charter tour bus.

Kanani and Vicki watched the closed tenders being lowered from the line of open lifeboats on the ship's deck above. Then they returned to their cabins to get ready.

* * *

Josh, his father, and Tank went to the lounge, where they were given blue tickets. Josh's mind was on all the complications in his life. He barely heard his father say that he had bus tickets for his party, which included the Kongs.

Mrs. Kong and Mrs. Fyfe entered the lounge, along with Kong, Kanani, and Vicki. They took seats opposite Josh and Tank. Mr. Ladd stepped over to the Kongs to explain the day's plans.

Tank leaned close to Josh and lowered his voice. "Kong is giving us dirty looks. I bet Kanani told him about yesterday . . . "

"Hold it!" Josh broke in. "I didn't make her cry! She chose to think that I didn't believe her."

"That won't make any difference to Kong. See the way he's grinding one fist into the other palm while his mother and your dad aren't looking at him? He's sending a message: 'Wait till I get you alone on shore.'"

"I know, but I can see that Kong and his family have green tickets. That means he won't be on the same boat with us. However, Dad's giving them their shore excursion tickets, so they will be on the same bus with us."

"I just hope we don't have to sit too near him," Tank replied ominously.

Josh pursed his lips thoughtfully. "Hmm. . . . Maybe that's exactly what I should do."

"What? Sit with Kong?"

"Sure! That would give me a chance to talk with him when he doesn't dare pound on me—not with his mother sitting close by."

"Kong's the last person in the world I want to talk to about anything, so why should you?"

"Because I want to know why he hates you and me so much. Maybe if we know that, we can work something out."

"Fat chance! Kong hates all haoles, not just us."

"But why? Don't you see, Tank? If I can get him to open up, maybe we can talk it through and he'll stop bothering us. Anyway, I've got to try."

"Not me! I want to live to a ripe old age!"

Just then the bearded man entered the lounge carrying a blue ticket. "Tank," Josh said in a low tone, "look who is going to be in the same boat with us."

Tank lifted his eyes to where Baxter Yount sat down near the rear double doors. At the same time, the red-haired man came in. He also held a blue ticket.

"Things are getting interesting," Tank whispered to Josh.

"Sure are! This is the first chance Yount has had to pass on the stolen disk. I wonder how he's going to do that, knowing that Mr. Tilford is going to be right behind him? Dad says that even if he is a federal agent, he has no authority in Mexico."

"I'll bet Stark has radioed local police to be waiting to arrest Yount. That way, they can also arrest whoever the buyer is."

"I hope we can see it happen," Josh said as the public-address system announced that all persons holding blue tickets should now make their way to the third deck.

Josh sighed with relief. "At least we'll beat Kong ashore."

"And then he'll try to beat up on us, especially if you try to talk to him on the bus," Tank said somberly.

"He's going to try that anyway, so I'm going to risk talking to him."

The boys and Mr. Ladd were among the last of sixty passengers to fill the bouncing tender. They took seats at the stern. Josh was relieved to see that the bearded Yount was seated at the bow and the red-haired Tilford was about halfway back. The tender headed for shore, filling the closed craft with diesel fumes.

The engines were too noisy to allow conversation, so Josh let his blue-eyed gaze drift away from the ship and across Puerto Vallarta. He had learned something about it yesterday in the lecture on board ship.

Puerto Vallarta's quarter of a million residents lived in a scenic city of red-tiled roofs and semitropical vegetation. The year-round temperature averaged in the eighties, reminding Josh of Hawaii. This similarity was further enhanced by the glistening beaches and sparkling bay and ocean waters. A number of Americans lived in a section called *Gringo Gulch**.

As the boat touched the small dock, Josh glanced around at several local people watching the passengers. Josh wondered which ones were the plainclothes police officers assigned to trail Yount.

Disembarkation was from the tender's stern, so Josh and Tank were the first ones off, followed by Mr. Ladd. He said, "You boys may look around here until the Kong family comes ashore. I'm going to make sure they get on our charter bus."

The boys nodded and turned their attention to Yount and Tilford while local taxi drivers pressed forward. In heavily accented English, the drivers called out, offering rides to various sight-seeing spots, shopping areas, and other attractions. Behind the taxis, small, old charter buses were lined up.

Josh and Tank deliberately held back so they could see both Yount and Tilford, while staying where Josh's dad could see them.

Some eager vendors called out about their wares. One said to a matronly woman walking beside the boys, "You want silver? Beautiful earrings, very cheap. Only fifteen dollars."

She shook her head. "*Muy caro. Muy caro.*"

Tank leaned close to whisper to Josh, "She means, 'Too expensive.' I remember hearing those words yesterday at the orientation meeting."

"Never mind that," Josh replied, suddenly tensing. "Yount's getting into that first taxi!"

"That means we can't follow him."

"No, but Tilford can." Josh pointed to where the red-haired man was getting into a second taxi. "I'm sure sorry we can't see what's going to happen with them."

"Me, too. We'll miss all the excitement when the local police move in on Yount as he passes that disk on. I just can't figure what Tilford's going to do."

"Well, whatever it is, it's out of our hands." Josh turned to look at a tender leaving the ship with another load of shore-bound passengers. "We've still got a chance to talk with Kong and his little sister."

"You're on your own, there, Josh. I'm not going near Kong. Neither am I going to let him get close to me."

"I'll talk to him, but I need your help with Kanani. She won't speak to me, but maybe if you can sit by her, you can clear up the misunderstanding she has . . . "

"Oh, no!" Tank broke in. "First of all, she can't be pried away from Vicki, and between the two of them, they'll either talk me to death or bore me stiff."

"That's better than having Kong thump on us."

Tank sighed. "Yeah, you're right. You're taking a worse risk talking to him."

Josh grinned. "Does that mean you'll do it?"

"Yeah, I guess so. But there's something I want you to tell me first."

"What's that?"

"What's the Spanish word for 'flowers'?"

"I don't know. Why do you ask?"

"Because I'm going to have to order some for your funeral after you talk to Kong."

Josh playfully punched his friend on the shoulder. Then they wandered off to the vendors' booths. The boys ignored broken-English invitations to buy souvenirs ranging from handmade jewelry to pottery to immense sombreros* decorated in vivid colors.

All the while, Josh watched tenders docking. Soon Mrs. Fyfe stepped ashore with Vicki, followed by Mrs. Kong, Kanani, and Kong. Josh watched his father move forward to greet them, then point toward the waiting buses.

"Good!" Josh exclaimed. "We're all going to be on the same bus. Now, remember, I'll try to sit next to Kong. You know what to do with Kanani."

"You're going to owe me big time for this," Tank warned.

Several minutes later, Josh deliberately stepped in behind Kong as he boarded the small bus. Kong didn't seem to notice until he took a window seat and Josh sat beside him on the aisle.

"Hey, you dumb haole!" Kong growled, keeping his voice low and glancing at his mother to make sure she couldn't hear him. "No sit! Kong keep all dis seat."

Josh gulped and tried to smile at the big kid. "I want to talk to you."

"Kong no talk Mainland malihini—'specially you." He started to shove Josh into the aisle.

"Wait!" Josh exclaimed, resisting the push. "Just answer one question. Okay?"

Kong shot another look at his mother coming down the aisle. He turned back to Josh. "Okay, one question."

Josh took a quick, deep breath. "Why do you hate Tank and me?"

"You haoles. Dat's why."

"What did we ever do to you, Kong?"

"Dat's two questions. You say only one. Now, go!"

Josh fought down the temptation to obey and made himself stay seated. He realized that this might be the only chance he ever had to find out something that might possibly end Kong's constant bullying.

Licking his lips, which had suddenly gone dry, Josh shook his head. "I'm not going until you tell me why you hate haoles, even if you beat up on me the first chance you get."

"Kong do dat anyhow," Kong said with a humorless smile.

"So why do you hate us, and especially Tank and me?"

Kong glared at Josh and clenched his big fists just as his mother lowered her considerable bulk into a seat across the aisle and one seat ahead. She said, "Kamuela, I'm glad to see that you and Josh are talking."

Kong gave her a weak smile before she turned away and started talking to Mrs. Fyfe. Kanani and Vicki were seated in front of the women, with Mr. Ladd and Tank in front of them. Tank turned around and spoke to the girls, but Josh couldn't hear what was said.

Josh breathed a bit easier, knowing that Kong wouldn't make a scene with his mother so close. Josh turned back to Kong. "Are you going to tell me?"

Kong's dark eyes suddenly blazed with inner fury. He took a deep breath and seemed about to explode with an angry answer. Then, abruptly, he opened his mouth and released the air in a mighty gust. His eyes lost their fierceness.

Josh was surprised to see a sudden moist brightness covering Kong's eyes. Josh tried not to stare. *Tears!* he thought. *He's got tears in his eyes!*

It was the most amazing thing Josh could imagine, but he forced himself to look away so as not to embarrass Kong. Josh asked in a soft voice, "Did haoles hurt you?"

Kong replied in a tone so low Josh almost missed the words: "Haoles kill makua kane*."

"Your father?"

Kong nodded, turning his massive head away so that the tears didn't show, but one slid out of the corner of his left eye and down his cheek. "Long time go, when Kong only keike kane*."

Josh exclaimed, "Oh, I'm really sorry, Kong! How did it happen?"

"Two haole men have big huhu* wit' makua kane. One night, after work, dey hide in cane field." Kong pointed his forefinger with the thumb up, then dropped it down on the finger. "Boom!"

Kong's big chest seemed seized with a convulsion, and he turned his face away.

Josh gently laid his hand on Kong's great biceps. "That's terrible!"

Kong's body shook for a moment before he suddenly whirled and glowered at Josh through misty, hurt eyes. "Kong little den. Kanani only baby." He jerked his head toward his mother. "Big pilikia* foh her. She forgive haoles who shoot. Not Kong! Never! Hate all haoles!"

Josh didn't know what to say in the face of such intense, long-lasting hatred, but he felt he had to say something. "I'm very sorry, Kong, but that's no reason to hate other people. I have friends who are white, brown, black, red, and yellow. Most people are good, no matter what their color, but a few are bad, and it has nothing to do with the color of their skins. So why hate me . . . ?"

Kong interrupted angrily. "Hate you an' Tank foh different reason!"

Josh cocked his head. "Oh? What reason is that?"

"You got makua kane! Kong no got daddy!"

Josh stared, not sure he understood. Slowly, facing Kong's scowl and angry, misty eyes, Josh asked, "You hate us because we have fathers?"

Kong nodded. "Not fair! You dumb Mainland malihinis got fathah. Take you places. Have fun. Come home night. Be whan beeg happy family! But Kong got only wahines*."

Josh tried to think of something to say, but he was too surprised.

Kong added, his voice heavy with pain, "Now you know, haole boy, but you not tell."

"Can't I even tell Tank?"

Kong started to shake his head, then shrugged. "Bes' friend, okay. Nobody else. Unnerstan'?"

Josh nodded as the local Mexican guide stood at the front of the bus and picked up a microphone. "*Buenos tardes*," he said. "My name: Pedro. I speak English leetle bit. Driver is Pepe. We show you Puerto Vallarta."

Josh saw Tank abruptly get up from his seat and hurry down the aisle.

Ignoring Kong, Tank leaned over to Josh and whispered, "Move to an empty backseat so we can talk right now! You won't believe what Kanani's up to!"

Chapter Nine

A CAT AND MOUSE GAME

While Pedro's voice continued over the public-address system, Josh slid into an empty seat at the back of the bus where Tank had moved.

"What's the matter?" Josh asked impatiently. "Kong was just telling me why he hates us so much."

"That'll wait," Tank replied, lowering his voice, although the bus was so noisy that nobody could have overheard. "Kanani's so mad at you for not believing her that she says she's going to tell the redheaded man that she saw Baxter Yount put something in your baggage."

Josh felt instant alarm, then shrugged. "Before today, that could have made a big difference. But this whole thing should be over when the police grab Yount as he tries to pass on that stolen disk."

"What if something goes wrong, and that doesn't happen?"

"There you go again, Tank! Always looking at the bad side."

"No, I'm not! Maybe this isn't the port where Yount is supposed to meet his contact to sell the disk. And what about

87

Tilford? We still don't really know for sure where he fits into this."

"That's true, and you could be right. If nothing changes from yesterday, Kanani could mess everything up."

"Yeah! Maybe Tilford doesn't care whether Yount gets arrested or not. He might just want the disk."

"That's possible," Josh admitted. "If Tilford wants to recover it, whether for himself or for the person who hired him, and he learns that it was in my bag . . . "

"He'll want it," Tank interrupted, "and you don't have it. But he might not believe you."

"And I can't tell him because of the promise we made to the security officer. We can't tell Kanani either." Josh sighed. "Let's hope the whole thing is over when we get back on the ship, so we can forget about it."

"What if it's not?" Tank asked.

"Then we'll just have to deal with it. Anyway, I have to get back to Kong. You won't believe why he hates us so much."

"Yeah? Why?"

"I'll tell you when we make our first stop. Right now, I hope that Kong won't stop talking to me after this interruption."

Josh returned to his seat beside the big bully, who silently stared out the window. He wouldn't even turn around to look at Josh.

Josh sighed and reluctantly turned his attention to the guide's friendly, humorous patter.

Josh barely noticed the drive along the seawall promenade, the cobblestone streets, the Cathedral of Our Lady of

Guadelupe*, and other sights.

The first chance to talk to Tank came when the bus stopped where passengers could stroll through tropical gardens. Kong stalked off by himself. Josh and Tank dropped behind the others, giving Josh time to tell Tank of his talk with Kong.

When Josh finished, Tank commented, "I never heard of anybody being mad at someone else just because they have a dad."

The conversation shifted to Tank's conversation with Kanani. Tank concluded by saying, "She told me that her brother can speak proper English if he wants. But he uses pidgin as a form of rebellion. His mom thinks he'll get over it."

"She must be a very tolerant mother."

"I suppose. And do you know why Kong pulls on those black gloves when he's about to punch somebody out?"

"To scare his victim more, I guess."

"No, it's because he won't dirty his hands on a haole kid."

All passengers returned to the bus for the trip down Puerto Vallarta's Gold Coast. Kong changed seats, so Josh had to sit with a heavyset woman who chattered endlessly about how beautiful the city was. Josh barely listened because of wondering what had happened to Yount and Tilford.

He found out soon after reboarding the ship. Kong stalked off without a word. Josh and Tank climbed to the top deck to look out over the city's skyline.

Suddenly, Josh sucked in his breath. "Look! Getting out of that last bus!"

"Mr. Yount! They didn't arrest him."

"They'd have no reason unless he tried to pass along that stolen disk. He obviously didn't do that. Now what?"

"Yeah! And where is Tilford? And Kanani? If she tells him . . ."

"I know!" Josh broke in. "I think we'd better find the security officer and ask him what happened."

The boys raced down the stairs without waiting for the elevators. They reached the fifth-deck stairwell, now filled with passengers.

Josh grabbed Tank's arm and said in a low voice, "Over there!" He pointed to where the red-haired man was just getting out of an elevator.

"Colby Tilford!" Tank exclaimed. "And Kanani and Vicki are pushing through the crowd, trying to follow him! I'll bet they're going to tell him about Kanani seeing Baxter Yount put that disk in your bag!"

"We can't let that happen!"

The boys ran after the girls.

* * *

Kanani and Vicki dodged through other passengers who were strolling or just standing and talking.

Kanani told Vicki, "After we tip Mr. Tilford off to where the bearded man hid whatever it was in Josh's bag, and Tilford recovers it, maybe there will be a reward and he'll split it with us."

"Wouldn't that be something?" Without waiting for a reply, Vicki asked, "What happens if the bearded man finds out we helped the agent get it back? He won't like it, and then we could be in danger."

"Josh is the one who's going to be in trouble, and it serves him right for not believing me."

The girls were finally through the crowds and gaining on the red-haired man, who was walking down a corridor. He turned a corner near the ship's stern and entered a stairwell.

Seconds later, when Kanani and Vicki reached that area, they stopped in surprise.

"He's gone!" Kanani exclaimed, turning rapidly to look around. "He must have gone out on the deck, but which side? You take that, and I'll take this."

Kanani finished checking first. She raced back through the stairwell area and out onto the port deck, where Vicki was standing, a bewildered look on her face.

"How could he have disappeared so fast?" Vicki asked.

Kanani pointed. "There are some iron doors with a sign that says *Keep Out—Crew Only*. He could have ducked in . . . "

She left her thought unfinished as Josh and Tank burst through the glass doors onto the deck.

"Whew!" Josh exclaimed, sliding to a stop. "I'm glad we caught you. We've got to talk."

"No, we don't!" Kanani snapped, turning up her nose and grabbing Vicki's hand. "Let's get away from here."

"Wait!" Josh called. "There's something you don't know."

"And there's something you don't know either!" Kanani called over her shoulder. "Maybe someday you'll wish you had believed me!"

The girls flounced off, leaving Josh and Tank standing

sheepishly as the ship's deep-throated blast announced immediate departure from Puerto Vallarta.

Glumly, the boys started looking for Dave Stark, the security officer, to ask what had happened on shore with Yount and Tilford. They phoned his extension but got no answer. There was nothing left but to walk around the ship in hopes of running into him.

Dusk was falling when the boys checked the ship's stern, where a shuffleboard game was in progress. A string of overhead white lights came on so the game could continue.

"Hey, you guys, come over here!" Micah called from a deck chair where he was watching some gray-haired people play shuffleboard.

Josh and Tank accepted Micah's invitation. They took chairs on either side of the other boy.

"How's your grandmother?" Josh asked.

"Not so hot. The ship's doctor has been treating her for seasickness, even though the sea's been very calm. Grandpa says it's just nerves and being scared because she's never been this far from home since she left Japan. She really hates traveling, but Grandpa thinks she'll be fine once we turn around and start back."

"I'd like to meet your grandparents," Josh replied.

"As soon as she's better, I'll introduce you."

Josh liked Micah. He was warm and friendly, although Josh had not seen him much except when he was with Kong. Josh asked, "How do you get along with Kong?"

Micah shrugged. "He's okay, but he doesn't like you two.

But I guess you know that."

Josh nodded, remembering how Kong's eyes had filled with tears on the bus when he told why he hated haoles.

Micah looked beyond Josh. "Here he comes now."

Josh turned a little apprehensively to watch the big boy as he clumped up in monstrous tennis shoes.

"You Mainland malihinis go," Kong growled without looking at them. He waved a huge arm toward the main part of the ship. "Micah, Kong play you whan game da kine shuffleboard, yeah?"

Micah nodded. "Okay, but let's let these two guys play with us."

"No," Kong growled. "Nobody but Kong an' Micah."

Josh and Tank said hasty good-byes to Micah and resumed their search for Dave Stark, eager to learn where Yount and Tilford had gone in the taxis.

* * *

Kanani and Vicki completed a search of the ship but found no sign of either Yount or Tilford. They even took the elevator to the lowest deck marked on the panel. It opened to the laundry room, where steam poured into the elevator.

"Let's try the promenade deck one more time," Kanani suggested. "Everybody walks along there sooner or later, so maybe he'll come along, too."

They pushed the button for the seventh deck. It stopped at the sixth deck, where an elderly woman got on. As the doors started to shut, Kanani caught a glimpse of Josh and Tank reflected in the mirrors behind the stairs.

"Wait!" she cried, reaching for the *Door Open* button, but it was too late. The doors finished closing and the elevator started up.

"What was that about?" Vicki asked.

Lowering her voice, Kanani explained, "I just saw Josh and Tank talking to one of those uniformed officers. He had those black boards on his shoulders."

"That means he's a security officer! My mother told me that's who they are. But why are the boys talking to one of them?"

"Let's find out." Kanani darted out as the elevator doors opened. She headed for the stairs.

* * *

The boys finally located Dave Stark, head of the ship's security division. He said that the bearded man, Baxter Yount, took a taxi to a downtown department store where the local plainclothes officers lost sight of him for about ten minutes.

Josh guessed, "So in that time, he could have passed along the disk without anyone seeing him."

"That's right," Stark agreed. "But if he did, by now whoever got the disk will know it's blank. That could make that other person angry. If this is an industrial espionage theft, as I suspect it is, then whoever received the blank disk will think Yount tried to rip them off. There's a chance that they might plan revenge on him."

"What kind of revenge?" Josh asked. He recalled with a shudder what the bearded man had once told him about somebody going overboard and never being seen again.

"Depends on how nasty the others are," Stark explained. "I don't expect any trouble on this ship, but who knows what might happen tomorrow when we dock again."

Josh asked, "What about the other man, Mr. Tilford?"

Stark replied, "The local authorities who followed him reported that he just drove around alone, sightseeing. He didn't talk to anybody except his taxi driver. That's the situation for now. It's not your concern, boys, so please stay out of harm's way."

"So nothing's changed," Josh summarized. He thanked Stark, and then both boys walked thoughtfully away.

* * *

Kanani and Vicki emerged from where they had been secretly watching Josh, Tank, and the security officer.

Kanani said fiercely, "I'm so disappointed that we couldn't hear what they were saying."

"Me, too. From the way they were talking in such low voices, you can be sure it was something important. I'm sure it was about those same men we're watching."

Kanani stared after Josh and Tank. "I wish we could get close."

"My mom says eavesdropping is wrong."

"I didn't say we should do that!"

"It sure sounded like it," Vicki replied.

"Well, you heard wrong."

"Why are you snapping at me?"

"Because I'm frustrated, that's why!"

Vicki replied with a faint smile, "Eavesdropping on the

boys could cure your frustration."

Kanani considered that. "I think you're right. Let's try it." She hurried after the boys, with Vicki following close behind.

* * *

Josh had trouble opening the stateroom door. "That's funny," he said, jiggling the key. "It doesn't seem to fit right."

"Let me try." Tank took the small key and carefully inserted it. "You're right," he commented. "It feels different from the last time. . . . There! I got it."

Josh retrieved his key and stepped inside, leaving the door open. Then he stopped in surprise.

"My bag!" He quickly bent to examine it where it lay open on the floor in front of the closet. "Dad wouldn't have done that."

"You're right! Somebody must have forced the lock to break in, and that's why the key wouldn't work right." Tank's usually slow voice speeded up with excitement. "Maybe Kanani *did* tell Mr. Tilford that she had seen Mr. Yount hide something in here, so Tilford broke in to get it."

Josh still knelt on the floor by the bag. "A secret government agent wouldn't break the law. So unless that's not what he really is, the only other possibility is that Yount somehow viewed that disk on shore, found out it was blank, and . . . "

"He broke in here again to search for the original," Tank interrupted. "But the security officer has it. Hey! Maybe when the Puerto Vallarta authorities lost sight of Yount in that department store, he went to the computer department and used one of their machines to view the disk. That's how he knows it's blank."

"That's possible, but if that's true," Josh said somberly, "then he's going to know I found the original disk. He'll think I've still got it and I substituted the blank one. He'll blame me, and he'll try to get it back."

Tank's eyes widened. "Mr. Yount will also know that you and I are always together, so he could come after both of us."

Josh turned toward the door. "We'd better go find my dad and tell him, and probably the security officer, too. If Mr. Yount thinks the girls are involved, they could be in danger, too."

* * *

Outside the open stateroom door, the frightened girls had heard everything. Vicki silently ran down the carpeted corridor. Kanani fled on tiptoes after her.

Chapter Ten

ADVENTURE IN ACAPULCO

Josh's father and Dave Stark worked out a plan. Several of the ship's security officers would dress as passengers and mingle with the others to better protect Josh, Tank, and the girls from the bearded Yount.

Another security detail would quietly keep both Yount and Tilford under surveillance. Another officer would dress as a cabin steward to stay where the Ladds' stateroom could be observed in case another break-in was attempted.

"Please understand," the ship's chief security officer concluded. "We don't tolerate trouble on this ship. However, if it starts, we quietly control it. That way, other passengers don't even suspect anything is going on, and they can enjoy their cruise. We want to make everything appear normal so the thief will make his next move and we can apprehend him without incident."

That night, Josh was disappointed when nothing happened. He was more hopeful the next day when the ship dropped anchor at Zihuatenejo, a small Mexican community.

Yount did not go ashore, but Tilford, the Ladds, the Kongs,

and the Fyfes did take the tenders. There was no bus tour, so everyone strolled in small groups along streets immediately adjacent to the bay.

Mindful of the security chief's warnings, the boys did not follow the red-haired Tilford. However, they did keep him in sight as they sauntered along streets made of interlocking tiles, unlike Puerto Vallarta's cobblestones.

Who is Mr. Tilford, really? Josh wondered. *And why did Mr. Yount stay on board today? Maybe because he found out in Puerto Vallarta that he has a blank disk, and he's going to try getting the original back from our stateroom. Well, he won't find it.*

Josh and Tank, trailing their group, stopped periodically to inspect countless souvenirs offered by Mexican vendors. These were much less aggressive than those at Puerto Vallarta.

Josh commented, "Mr. Yount is staying on the ship. We should soon find out if he knows he's got a blank disk instead of the original one he hid in my bag."

"Yeah. While all of us are gone, he'll have a chance to break into our cabin again and make a thorough search for the original disk."

"If he does," Josh added, "the security people will grab him. But if he doesn't try, then that means he thinks that he's got the original disk. Unless, of course, he passed it on at Puerto Vallarta when the local cops lost him for a while."

"And if Mr. Yount doesn't try breaking in, then that means that he wasn't the one who broke in yesterday. But if he didn't, who did?"

"The only other logical person is Mr. Tilford."

"A federal agent wouldn't do that."

"We don't know whether that's what he is. Remember that Mr. Stark said he hadn't been able to learn anything about Mr. Tilford except that he seems to be who he said he was, and that he is in investments."

Tank shook his head. "If that's not his cover*, then who could he be?"

"I don't know. But tomorrow's stop in Acapulco is the last port the ship is making before heading home. So let's keep a close eye on Mr. Tilford right now."

The boys watched the red-haired man give some change to a young Indian boy holding out his hand, silently begging from American tourists. The little boy took the money to his tiny Indian mother. Josh noticed that she and other Indian women were under five feet tall and looked distinctively different from Mexican women. Many of the men seemed to have gold teeth or fillings.

Tilford didn't speak to them or to anyone except a few vendors offering their wares from tiny carts or stalls. However, the red-haired man didn't buy anything and returned to the ship after less than an hour.

"I guess we've seen enough here," Josh commented. "Let's catch the next tender back and check things out."

On board, Josh and Tank hurried to their stateroom. The boys looked at each other knowingly as they passed a new room steward with his cart of bedding in the corridor. The boys realized he was really a security officer, although he gave them no indication of that.

A quick check of the cabin showed there had been no forced entry and nothing had been disturbed.

"Now what?" Tank asked.

"We wait for tomorrow at Acapulco. It's our last port, so Mr. Yount has to meet his contact and pass on the disk—*if* he didn't do that in Puerto Vallarta."

"And *if* he didn't discover that he has a blank disk because you found the original and gave it to the ship's security officer."

"True. This is also Mr. Tilford's last chance to act, so we should find out who he really is."

"One thing still bothers me: who tried to break into our cabin yesterday?"

"We should find out tomorrow. Then you and I can breathe easier. Let's go watch the ship leave."

Josh and Tank were on the elevator when it stopped at the seventh deck and Micah got on. He said he was going to the top deck to watch the ship sail.

"So are we," Josh replied, then asked, "How's your grandmother?"

"Better, thanks. Grandpa thinks it's because she knows that this time tomorrow night we'll be on our way home."

"What would they have done if she became really sick while we were out on the ocean?" Tank inquired.

"The ship's doctor said that if we were in American waters, the Coast Guard would send a helicopter for her." Micah paused, then added, "You've seen the shuffleboard deck at the ship's stern. Those overhead lights would be removed, and the chopper would hover over that section of the deck. The ship would slow down but not stop."

"Why not?" Tank wanted to know.

"The doctor said the ship would lose headway and be hard to control if it stopped completely," Micah explained. "So the chopper would lower a cable with a kind of basket called a Stokes. Grandma would be put on it and pulled up into the chopper. Then it would fly her to the nearest hospital."

"Let's hope it's not necessary," Josh said.

Tank asked, "What happens in foreign waters where there isn't a Coast Guard station?"

Micah replied, "The doctor said the ship puts into the nearest port. The patient goes by ambulance to the closest hospital. After that, she'd have to fly home."

The boys fell silent as the ship's great whistle sounded, announcing immediate departure for Acapulco.

* * *

Kanani and Vicki stood inside the big double doors on the top deck and watched the three boys leaning over the rail. Kanani felt the ship's engines gaining speed so that there was a slight vibration under her feet. At the same time, a huge black cloud of smoke erupted from the ship's stack.

"Go on, Kanani," Vicki urged. "We've got to tell them what we overheard."

"Wait until that other kid has gone."

Vicki threw her hands up in mock despair. "If you won't do it right now, I will."

"Oh, all right!" Kanani snapped. "Stop nagging." She

started to open the doors leading to the deck where Josh and Tank stood.

"Hey, girls!" A man's voice behind them made them whirl about. The red-haired man stood by the elevator.

"Wonder what he wants?" Vicki asked softly.

"Let's go find out."

Vicki sighed and followed Kanani to where Tilford waited.

He looked directly at Vicki and smiled. "Young lady, I keep thinking about something you said the other day. Why do you think I'm a secret government agent?"

Vicki looked at Kanani. "Because she saw you trailing that bearded man after he hid something in someone's suitcase."

Tilford turned to Kanani. "I'm sorry to disappoint you," he said gently. "But I'm definitely not a federal agent."

Kanani protested, "But you were following that bearded man right after we boarded the ship! I saw him hide a disk in Josh Ladd's bag there by the elevator and then run onto the deck. Seconds later, you showed up and asked if I'd seen him. I pointed the way he'd gone."

Kanani saw something flicker across Tilford's eyes before he said, "You must have me mixed up with someone else. I didn't follow anybody, and I first saw you that time by the elevator when both of you were together."

"But . . . ," Kanani began.

Tilford cut her off. "I'm sorry, you were mistaken."

He turned and strode rapidly down the corridor.

Kanani stared after him. She assured Vicki, "I'm positive that he's the same man . . . "

"And now," Vicki interrupted, "Mr. Tilford knows about everything. You just told him about the disk and its being in Josh Ladd's bag!"

Kanani's hand flew to her mouth and her eyes opened wide. "Oh! I did, didn't I?"

"Yes, you did. Anyway, you've been planning to tell him for days. Now it's done."

"Vicki, I'm scared! What if he really isn't a secret agent?"

"What does it matter?"

"Well, now he knows about Josh and the bag, and that we know something strange is going on. Besides, I saw something in Mr. Tilford's eyes that bothers me."

"You're just scaring yourself."

"I don't think so. There was something in his eyes. Something . . . "

"Stop it! You're scaring me, too. Let's go find the boys and tell them everything."

"I'll tell them first thing in the morning," Kanani said miserably, looking in the direction in which Tilford had gone. "Oh, Vicki, I sure hope I haven't done something terribly wrong!"

* * *

Josh awakened the next morning to find the ship snugged up alongside a long concrete dock at Acapulco.

Mr. Ladd had already left the cabin, so Josh roused his sleepy-headed best friend. "Rise and shine, Tank," Josh said cheerfully. "Today's the deadline for things to happen. Tonight we'll be on our way back to the United States."

The boys dressed, talking excitedly about what might happen when the bearded man tried to pass on the stolen disk. Then Josh and Tank walked out onto the open deck to have the buffet-style breakfast. The area was crowded, with almost all the tables taken.

"There's Kanani and Vicki," Josh said as the fragrance of bacon and coffee drifted to his nose. "Hey! They're motioning for us to join them."

Exchanging curious glances with each other, the boys approached the girls.

"I've got something to tell you, Josh," Kanani began, shoving aside a napkin on which she had been drawing. "Please sit down. Vicki, maybe you and Tank could get in line and bring Josh whatever he wants."

Tank said with mock pain, "I know when I'm not wanted. Come on, Vicki. Let's leave these two alone."

When they had gone, Josh looked across at Kanani, but she avoided his eyes. He glanced at the napkin. It had a sketch of a little Indian boy begging for coins.

Josh commented, "You're a very good artist."

"Thanks." She forced herself to think how to tell Josh that she and Vicki had eavesdropped outside of the Ladds' cabin. But she had to know more about what they had overheard.

"You could have won this trip with your drawings."

Kanani reacted by crumpling the napkin and throwing it on the table. "I don't want to talk about it!"

Josh stared in surprise, but she looked away, refusing to meet his eyes. A realization swept over Josh. He blurted, "It was your drawing that won the contest, wasn't it? But your brother took the credit, didn't he?"

"I didn't say that!"

Josh slowly nodded. "But that's what happened."

She looked at him, her eyes bright. "Vicki and I did something wrong yesterday," she said, abruptly changing the subject. "No, I'm the one—I did something wrong the other day, and I just made it worse."

She confessed to listening outside the Ladds' stateroom door and learning about the disk that Stark now had.

Josh stared in open-mouthed surprise as Kanani continued. "That was a bad enough thing to do, but there's more. Remember when I told you that I had seen the bearded man hide something in your bag, then run away just before the red-headed man came along?"

"I remember."

"Well, yesterday I accidentally told Mr. Tilford about it being a disk that I saw Mr. Yount hide in your bag."

Josh scowled across the table at Kanani while trying to sort out his feelings. He was angry at her for eavesdropping and learning things he had promised the security chief that he would keep secret. But Josh was also concerned because now Tilford also knew that Yount had hidden the disk in Josh's baggage.

"I'm awfully sorry, Josh," Kanani said when he still sat in silence. She added quickly, "What's going on? Are we all in danger now?"

Josh slowly roused himself. "Let's hope not, but we don't

really know for sure. We just think it all has to happen today in Acapulco."

"Then would it be all right if Vicki and I went ashore with you and Tank today?"

Josh hesitated, knowing that he was in big trouble for talking to Kanani. Could it be any worse if Kong saw them on the bus? *Besides,* Josh comforted himself, *Dad said he had booked all of us on this tour, and maybe the girls will be safer with Tank and me.*

"Sure," Josh assured Kanani. "It'll be fine."

* * *

Later, Josh took his video camera and followed Tank, the girls, Kong, Micah, and the adults. They left the ship from the third deck, stepping directly onto the dock. Mr. Ladd led his party across to the curb, where a long line of cabs and small buses waited.

Many local taxi drivers rushed up, aggressively offering their services.

Mr. Ladd replied, "No, *gracias**," and led his party toward the buses.

Josh kept looking around, hoping to see Yount or Tilford among the hundreds of passengers milling about on the sidewalk.

I guess we won't get to see what happens, Josh mused, and entered the nearest bus, following Tank, Kanani, and Vicki. The girls took a seat just behind Josh and Tank. Kong sat across the aisle from the boys but didn't look at them. Josh hadn't had an opportunity to follow up on their conversation, but he kept hoping to do so.

Josh was grateful that Kong had not really bothered him or Tank too much. He hoped that his talk with Kong might have helped, too.

Most of all, Josh had a sense of excitement, knowing that this was the final day when Yount would have to pass along the stolen disk. Whoever Tilford was, and whatever he planned to do, would probably be revealed today, too. Josh told himself that he would be glad when it was over.

As the guide introduced himself as José, Josh lowered his voice to Tank. "Have you seen Mr. Yount or Mr. Tilford?"

"No, but they're not our responsibility," Tank replied. "Let's relax and enjoy the ride."

José had a friendly, humorous patter that he mixed with brief descriptions of sights along the route. Other buses followed through the picturesque city.

There were stops for shopping where Kanani and Vicki stayed with Josh, Tank, and Mr. Ladd. Mr. Ladd had studied Spanish in college, so he did some translating and bargaining for Mrs. Kong and Mrs. Fyfe. Kong wandered off by himself on each stop.

As the bus caravan headed out of town for the last stop before returning to the ship, Josh told Tank, "I sure wish I knew whether that disk was passed and Yount arrested."

"Yeah, and I wish I knew how Tilford fits into all this. I guess we'll just have to wait to find out."

The boys fell silent, listening to their guide's explanation of what they were going to see. Acapulco's world-famous high divers would plunge 135 feet from rocky cliffs into a narrow channel. Each dive had to be carefully timed so incoming surges from the sea would give enough depth for diver safety.

There had been no fatalities in sixty years, although two divers had been blinded. One lost his sight from the water's impact on an optic nerve. Another diver was blinded from a Popsicle stick that someone had carelessly tossed into the water.

The buses stopped in a large parking lot overlooking the dive site. As the passengers got off, Kanani urged, "Hurry up, you guys, so we can find a good place to see." She and Vicki slipped through the older passengers heading toward the cliffs.

Kong lagged behind, falling into step between Josh and Tank. "You got stink ear*," he growled, glaring at Josh. "Kong tell you no talk da kine sistah. Now Kong break you' face soon." Kong increased his speed, gaining on the girls.

Tank moaned, "I was afraid that would happen."

Josh felt sick. "I had to talk to her. You know that."

He walked on, his spirit suddenly heavy. He looked for either Yount or Tilford, but with no success. Kanani and Vicki motioned for him and Tank to join them at a rail overlooking the channel below, but the boys pretended not to see. They moved to the left side, toward the road.

Josh removed the lens cap and aimed his camera up at the first diver, who approached the end of the high cliff. He stood over the surging channel far below and raised both hands high over his head. He held that position for several seconds, giving Josh a moment to pan across the upturned faces of the expectant crowd.

At their far left, Josh caught a taxi speeding into the parking lot. In the viewfinder, the bearded passenger in the back-seat could be seen leaning out the window. But he didn't even glance up at the diver. Instead, he looked behind Josh, who let out a startled exclamation: "Hey! Mr. Yount is just arriving in a taxi!"

Both boys watched the bearded man leap out of the cab almost before it stopped. He hurried toward the back of a parked bus. A local man stepped out from behind it and moved to meet Yount.

Josh whispered to Tank, "I'm going to shoot this."

"Don't let him see you! It could be dangerous!"

Josh didn't seem to hear. He crouched low, clutching his video camera. Keeping the buses between himself and the two men, he darted back across the parking lot.

Chapter Eleven

TERROR IN THE DARK

Josh dashed between two lines of buses, holding the video camera close to his chest. Behind him, he heard the crowd break into applause. He guessed that the diver had successfully leaped off the top of the cliff. Josh didn't dare risk looking back.

He slowed as he neared the back end of the last two buses. Cautiously, he poked his head out and eased the camera to his eye. It automatically focused, so he pushed the thumb button. The camera's red light came on and the built-in microphone began recording sounds.

In the viewfinder, Josh clearly saw both men in the fore-ground, with Yount's taxi driver waiting behind them. Yount faced a well-dressed stranger who looked like an American. Josh clearly heard the man's angry voice.

"What do you mean, somebody switched the disk?" he demanded.

"Just that," Yount replied, "and lower your voice."

"Don't tell me what to do! If you're trying to get more money or plan to sell to someone else . . . "

"No, no!" Yount shook his head vigorously. "Nothing like

111

that. Really! Somebody on that ship switched the original disk and substituted this one. Here, take it. You'll see it's blank, just as I did when I took it to a department store in Puerto Vallarta and viewed it on a demonstrator computer."

"We're not interested in a blank disk or in your story, Yount. We paid handsomely for the information you were to deliver to us. Now, hand it over, or . . . "

"I tell you, I don't have it!"

"Who does?"

"I don't know," Yount protested. "But there are only two possibilities. A redheaded guy calling himself Corby Tilford has been following me all the way from Los Angeles. Maybe he got it. If not, the only other possibility is that a kid found it . . . "

"Shut up, Yount!" The stranger's voice had become hard and cold. "The deal was to deliver it here and now. You wouldn't want to have an 'accident,' would you? You might not be as lucky as those divers." He glanced toward the cliffs, then stopped dead still at the sight of Josh.

"Hey, kid! What are you doing with that camera?"

Josh didn't even take time to push the *Off* button. He lowered the camera and dashed back between the buses, hearing the stranger running after him.

He also heard another voice. "*Alto*! Policia*!*"

Josh kept going, hearing other male voices and more running footsteps behind him. Josh passed the bus nearest the dive site in time to glimpse the second diver sail gracefully from his high cliff and plunge toward the water below.

At the same time, tires squealed and a motor raced wildly. The taxi shot past the buses, rocked crazily, seemed about to roll over, then straightened out and roared back down the road toward the city.

* * *

Late that afternoon, weary from all the excitement, Josh and Tank stood alone on the top deck, watching the last passengers return to the ship.

Yount had escaped in his taxi but had not returned to his stateroom, according to the ship's security chief, Dave Stark. Josh's videocassette had been taken as evidence because Stark said it established a conspiracy to sell stolen American industrial secrets in a foreign country. Yount's Acapulco contact had been arrested, but he refused to tell the police anything.

"What bothers me now," Josh confided to Tank as the ship gave a single loud, long blast that echoed across the hills ringing the city, "is how Tilford fits into all this, and where Mr. Yount is now."

"I wish I knew, too," Tank replied.

Both boys leaned over the rail to see the ship's crew begin removing the side rails from the folding metal gangplank. At the same time, a middle-aged couple hurried wearily across a small park next to the docked ship. The crew waited until the man and woman entered the ship, then the gangplank was raised and secured.

"They almost missed the boat," Tank commented.

"It was close, all right," Josh agreed.

Josh raised his eyes for another look at Acapulco. It was a

beautiful city, with the hills, the tropical vegetation, and the bay leading to the Pacific Ocean.

Moments later, the *Far Horizons* inched straight out from the dock. Seawater churned, showing that the ship's thrusters were shoving the craft sideways into the channel. Josh hurriedly glanced over the dock, but there was no sign of the bearded man.

Josh observed, "I think Yount missed the boat."

"Great! The danger is over. Dave Stark has the disk, and now we don't have to worry about Yount. We should have a nice, pleasant voyage home, except for Kong."

"I hope you're right, but I'd still like to talk to Kong some more. Now that I know why he hates all haoles, and especially us, I think the ice is broken with him."

Tank warned somberly, "The only thing that's going to be broken is your head, and probably mine, too."

Josh thought that was possible, but he didn't want to dwell on it. He said, "I still can't figure how Mr. Tilford fits into this."

The boys wandered back into the ship's interior, where Tank decided he wanted to go swimming. Josh didn't feel like doing that, so Tank went to get his trunks.

Josh wandered around the decks. He found Kong and Micah just finishing a shuffleboard game. Summoning his courage, Josh greeted both boys, then turned to Kong.

"I'd like to talk with you, Kong," Josh said.

The big bully scowled. "Whassa mattah you, haole boy? You not see dat Kong have fun wit' friend Micah?"

Micah said, "It's okay, guys. I've got to check on my grandmother." He hurried toward the doors leading to the ship's interior.

Josh stood awkwardly facing Kong. "Uh," Josh began, "I've been thinking about what you said the other day on the bus. I mean, about losing your father . . . "

"Kong don't need no fathah!" he interrupted. "Kong don't need no malihini hangin' 'round neither. Go!"

Every fiber in Josh's being urged him to leave, but he gulped and stood his ground. "Just give me a minute."

Kong's hands curved into gigantic fists. He glowered at Josh, then looked beyond him and spoke to someone coming up behind Josh.

"What you want, huh?"

Josh turned to see Kanani standing there. "Mom wants you," she said.

Josh tried to not sigh with relief as Kong stepped past him, muttering more threats under his breath.

Kanani motioned for Josh to wait. She watched her brother until he had gone through the doors into the ship. Then she looked up at Josh, her brown eyes soft.

"Don't be mad at Kamuela," she said quietly. "Mom told me she overheard a little of what he told you on the bus the other day. I mean about our daddy."

"I'm sorry," Josh replied sincerely. "I can imagine how much it would hurt me to lose my dad."

"Thank you." Kanani paused, then added, "Mom says she thinks Kamuela regrets that he even told you anything on the bus. She says that now he may try harder than ever to be tough so you won't think he has a soft side."

Josh hesitated before asking, "What about you?"

"Right now I just want to tell you why Mom wants to see Kamuela." She took a breath, then continued, "She found out that I drew the picture that won the contest your dad's paper sponsored. I didn't tell her. Something that Kamuela said tipped her off."

"What's she going to do about it?"

"She said that she'd pay whatever the cruise cost because Kong lied to her. Now she's ashamed because of what your father must think of her and us kids."

Josh was silent for a moment. He was sure that Mrs. Kong didn't have enough money to pay for what the cruise had cost, but he didn't mention that. He had an uncomfortable feeling that Kong might be meaner than ever after his mother scolded him.

The melodic five-tone dinner gong sounded, giving Josh an opportunity to end the conversation. "I guess we should eat," he said, turning toward the ship's doors.

Kanani fell into step with Josh, who decided that since Kong already planned to beat up on him, it wouldn't be any worse if he and Kanani walked to dinner together.

She said, "Your dad told my mother a little of what happened after Vicki and I saw you running and some guy chasing you. What can you tell me?"

Josh briefly filled in the details and said, "What puzzles me is why the other man, Mr. Tilford, wasn't anywhere around during all this."

"I don't know. But he's back on board, although I haven't seen Mr. Yount."

Josh's mind flashed back to when he had first seen Tilford enter the terminal at San Pedro. Josh was sure that the red-haired man was then following Yount. Yount had hidden from Tilford. When the ship docked at Puerto Vallarta, Yount left in a taxi with Tilford following.

"I don't know," Josh confessed as they approached the dining table. "He's a mystery, isn't he?"

Tank, waiting at the table with Mr. Ladd, Mrs. Fyfe, and Vicki, raised his eyebrows as Josh approached with Kanani. Tank whispered, "You pupule, walking around with Kong's little sister after what he said today?"

"Tell you later," Josh said, unfolding his napkin.

Vicki announced, "Mrs. Kong and her son won't be down for dinner. She called on the phone to ask us to please excuse them. Didn't say why."

Kanani added, "It's nothing to worry about."

Everyone sat down just as Dave Stark, the security chief, made his way through the bustling stewards and busboys. He leaned over Mr. Ladd's shoulder and whispered something. Josh joined everyone in staring until his father stood and motioned for Josh to stand, too.

Tank asked, "What's going on?"

"I don't know," Josh replied. He excused himself and followed his father and Dave Stark out of the dining room into the nearest stair tower.

"Sorry to disturb your dinner," Stark said, dropping his voice, although no one was around. He looked straight at Josh. "I thought you should know that the disk found in your baggage has disappeared from my property room."

"What?" Mr. Ladd exclaimed.

"I don't see how it's possible, but it's gone," Stark explained. "We don't even know for sure when it happened. My preliminary investigation indicates it probably happened today, although it could have happened before we docked at Acapulco. So that means Yount could have had it when he left the ship today."

Josh protested, "But if he had done that, why would he have met with the man in Acapulco and claim he didn't have it?"

"He might have sold it to someone else for more money, although I don't know why he would have then risked meeting the original intended buyer. I checked his cabin. The steward said he hadn't seen Yount since Acapulco."

"I think he missed the ship," Josh said and explained why.

"If he did have the original disk and sold it to somebody else," Stark explained, "he probably caught the first flight from Acapulco. He would want to get far away as fast as possible with all the money he would have received. But I don't think that's what happened."

Mr. Ladd asked, "What do you think happened?"

"I think the redheaded man, Tilford, has it."

Josh said, "He's not some kind of undercover officer trying to recover the disk from Mr. Yount?"

"Tilford's no cop," Stark replied. "That much I've learned

by radio intelligence. But just who he really is, we don't yet know."

Josh asked, "You think Mr. Tilford stole it and then passed it along to someone in Acapulco today while everybody was watching the other man?"

"It's a possibility," Stark admitted.

"If that happened," Mr. Ladd said thoughtfully, "he would have sold it for cash, so he'll have that on him, and he's still on board. I saw him just before dinner."

"You could search his room!" Josh exclaimed.

Stark shook his head. "Not without probable cause. At this point, I don't have that. All I have is a vague possibility."

"Then search him when he goes ashore!" Josh cried.

"Same problem," Stark replied. "No probable cause."

He shrugged. "We'll have a few days to figure out the best course of action. Meanwhile, of course, all this must be kept very hush-hush."

"Except for telling my friend Tank?" Josh asked. "He didn't say a word before, and he won't now."

Stark nodded. "But nobody else."

Josh and his father returned to the dinner table, where Mr. Ladd discreetly fended off questions from Kanani and Vicki. Josh knew that Tank was bursting to know what was going on, but both boys contained themselves until dinner was over.

When the boys stood alone on the promenade deck, a pale moon had risen, making a rippling bridge across the otherwise totally dark ocean. Josh leaned against the railing and retold all that Stark had said.

"Hmm," Tank mused, gazing out across the Pacific. "What if Mr. Tilford really stole the disk from the security office but still has it?"

"Why would he do that?"

"Maybe he had a buyer back in the United States, and he followed Mr. Yount to get the disk back, but when you found it, that wrecked his plans for a while."

Josh admitted, "Kanani did tell him that I had found a disk hidden in my bag. Tilford would probably guess that we had turned it in to security."

"Yeah! So he must have waited for the right time . . . "

"Wait!" Josh held up his hand. "Even if we're right, how could Tilford get the disk off this ship? There are no more stops until Los Angeles."

"He must know that he's going to be suspected, and either his cabin would be searched or he would be when he gets off the ship in Los Angeles. So if he has the disk, he must have planned a way to get away with it."

"How?" Josh challenged.

Tank shrugged. "I don't know. But you always were good at solving mysteries. Let's see you do that now."

Josh pondered that as he turned away from the rail to reenter the ship's superstructure. Then he stopped.

"There's Kanani and Vicki," he said, lowering his voice. "If they see us, they'll want to ask again about why Dave Stark came to the table tonight."

The boys turned, hurried down the promenade deck toward the stern, and ducked inside at the first doors.

* * *

Kanani and Vicki, alone on the lighted deck, stepped over to the rail where the boys had been moments before. "I sure hoped we could find Josh and Tank," Kanani said wistfully. "I'd sure like to know what's going on."

"Me, too! I'm dying to know what was so important that the security man came to the table."

"It has to have something to do with either or both of those men, Mr. Yount or Mr. Tilford," Kanani mused. She turned and idly looked around at the sound of the double doors opening. "I think Josh and Tank are hiding from us so they won't have to tell. . . . Don't look now!"

"Why not?" Vicki asked, starting to turn around.

Kanani grabbed her friend's arm hard and stopped the turn. "Just wait a minute!" she whispered.

The girls stood silently while a man's footsteps sounded on the deck, moving toward the bow.

When they had faded away, Kanani asked in a low, excited voice. "Did you see him?"

"How could I? You blocked my view."

"It doesn't matter! That was Mr. Yount, but I hardly recognized him because he's shaved off his beard."

Vicki stiffened in alarm. "You sure? I heard he missed the ship. Besides, why would he have shaved off his beard?"

"I don't know, but I'm going to try finding out. Come on, let's follow him."

"Oh, no! It's dark down at that end of the ship."

"Stay here if you want, but I'm going after him." Kanani

rose on her tiptoes and started running down the deserted deck the way the man had gone.

When she neared the unlighted area where the deck narrowed and the rail came within about three feet of the superstructure, Kanani stopped. She looked back. Vicki was still standing where she had been.

Taking a deep breath, Kanani moved deeper into the dense shadows. She heard only the hiss of the waves far below as the ship's bow cut through the black waters.

Then she heard something else. She stopped, her heart thudding in sudden fear. She peered into the darkness all around, but saw nothing. Then she heard it again and realized that someone else was there with her.

She thought, *I'd better get out of . . .*

She turned back just as a big hand clamped across her mouth and a powerful arm encircled her body. She tried to scream, but made only a muffled sound as she was lifted off her feet.

Chapter Twelve

SEARCH THE SHIP!

With her feet jerked off the deck, Kanani struggled violently. She kicked and twisted, vainly trying to break free of the restraining arm that encircled her waist and the big hand clamped across her mouth. She couldn't breathe, and her panic made her heart beat wildly.

Her captor whispered hoarsely in her ear, "Calm down and listen to me. I don't want to hurt you. I just want to talk. If you'll promise not to scream, I'll take my hand off your mouth. Okay?"

The frenzied need to breathe made Kanani agree, so she nodded. She felt Yount's fingers slowly open across her mouth, but they weren't removed. She prepared to suck in a breath to scream, but he seemed to sense that, for the hand clamped down again.

"Don't even think it!" he hissed, his breath hot against her cheek. "Now, will you be quiet and listen?"

Her urgent need for air again forced her to nod. At the same time, she vaguely heard Vicki calling to her from the lighted part of the deck. Kanani thought only of escaping her desperate plight. This time, when her feet touched the deck, she would try getting away.

Yount kept his left arm about Kanani but eased his right hand slightly away from her mouth. "Where's that disk?"

Kanani protested, "I don't know . . . "

"Don't give me that!" The fingers again tightened against her mouth, bruising her lips. "I'm desperate, so you'd better tell me where it is or . . . " He lifted her bodily and took a step toward the ship's rail.

* * *

Josh and Tank entered through the double doors near the ship's stern and stopped in the deserted stairwell.

Tank grinned with satisfaction. "Well, I guess we gave those girls the slip."

"We sure did," Josh replied with an edge of concern to his voice. He turned to look back at the doors leading to the deck. "I wish they wouldn't wander around out there alone this time of night."

"Ah," Tank scoffed, "there's no danger anymore. Yount missed the ship at Acapulco, and the security people are keeping an eye on Tilford."

"Just the same," Josh replied, moving back toward the doors where he and Tank had entered, "maybe we should keep an eye on them."

"They'll be all right. Let's go do something."

"In a minute. I'm going to take a peek at them."

Josh carefully opened one door and stuck his head out. He saw Vicki facing away from him and frantically calling toward the dark area of the ship's bow.

"Tank, something's wrong!" Josh exclaimed. He shoved the door wide open and stepped out onto the deck. He heard Vicki's frightened cries.

"Kanani, why don't you answer? You're scaring me!"

Josh sprinted down the deck toward Vicki. "Where is she?" he called.

Vicki pointed toward the bow. "She thought she saw Mr. Yount, so she followed him! Now she won't answer . . . "

"I'll go check," Josh interrupted, nearing her. "Tank!" he called over his shoulder. "Hurry up!"

Josh dashed past the frightened Vicki without stopping. He heard Tank running behind him. Ahead, Josh discerned a shadowy outline in the darkened area where the ship's rail and superstructure came within about three feet of each other.

"Kanani?" he called. "Are you there?"

Josh heard a muffled cry. At the same instant, he glimpsed the shadowy outline become two people. A man darted away out of the darkness, heading for the bow. The remaining form became a girl. She staggered weakly toward Josh just as the man rounded the superstructure's far end and disappeared around the prow.

"Josh! Thank God you came!" Kanani cried, stumbling into the light. She threw her arms around his neck and collapsed against him, sobbing uncontrollably.

Tank arrived, breathing hard from running. "What happened?"

"I don't know yet, but I saw someone running away. Here,

help me get her onto one of those deck chairs." When Josh saw Vicki approaching timidly, he shouted, "Go get some help. Call security! Hurry!"

* * *

It took Josh's and Tank's combined efforts to calm Kanani down enough to understand the story she sobbed out. Josh had most of it straight when Vicki arrived with Dave Stark. Vicki put her comforting arms about Kanani while Josh explained to the security officer.

"As near as I could make out, Mr. Yount had shaved off his beard, but Kanani's sure that's who grabbed her when she followed him into that darkened area." Josh pointed, then continued, "Kanani said he put his hand over her mouth . . . "

"Like this!" Kanani interrupted, demonstrating. "Oh, I was so scared!"

"It's all right now," the officer assured her. "Do you think you can finish telling me what happened?"

Kanani took a couple of deep breaths before nodding. "I'll . . . try."

"Then go ahead, please," Stark urged.

"Well," Kanani began, her voice trembling, "he started dragging me toward the rail. I thought he was going to throw me overboard." She shuddered, then continued, "While he was carrying me, he whispered that when the ship sailed out of Los Angeles, he hid a little disk in a bag left in front of the elevator.

"He said, 'As I left, I looked back and saw you looking at the same bag. I also saw a redheaded man speak to you.'"

"Mr. Tilford," Josh guessed.

"That's right," Kanani agreed. "Mr. Yount told me that he saw me point in the direction he had gone, so he ran off, figuring that the redheaded man was right behind him. Mr. Yount said he planned to come back later and get the disk from Josh's bag. By then, it was gone."

Kanani flashed a tearful smile at Josh. "Then he came along and saved me." She turned to look up at the security officer. "Mr. Yount is an awful person! Will you catch him, please?"

"He can't get off the ship, so we'll find him," Stark replied. He spoke into his portable radio, asking to have two other security officers come to the promenade deck, port side, and bring the ship's doctor with them. Then Stark turned back to Kanani. "You're safe now. Finish telling us what happened."

Kanani tried but broke into tears again.

Josh said to the security officer, "She told me that later Yount got the disk out of my bag. But he became suspicious. So when he stopped at Puerto Vallarta, he took a taxi to a department store. He borrowed a computer, played the disk, and found it was blank. He had seen the original in Los Angeles and knew that someone switched disks on the ship."

Kanani said, "That's right. He said he naturally suspected Josh because the disk had been in his bag. Mr. Yount tried to find the original disk before he got to Acapulco, where he was to deliver it."

Kanani wiped her eyes with the back of her hand. "He also told me that he had been offered a lot of money—half paid in

L.A. and the rest to be paid in Acapulco—and he was afraid of what they'd do to him if he just didn't show up, even though he didn't have the right disk anymore."

Stark nodded. "I can guess the rest. If the contact there hadn't seen you with your camera, Josh, Yount might not have lived long. When the contact man chased you, Yount escaped in the taxi. He shaved somewhere, then came back on the ship. He had his ID card, but nobody recognized him."

Kanani added, "He hid out and watched for me in that dark place."

"But why?" Vicki interrupted. "What did he want?"

"Don't you see?" Kanani replied, then turned to Josh. "He said that he had seen me talking to you on the ship. He recognized you when you were taking pictures of him in Acapulco. He wanted me to find out what you'd done with the disk and get it back for him.

"Otherwise, he said, the people who hired him will probably be waiting for him in Los Angeles to finish him off. He told me that he was desperate, and I had to tell him where the disk was and help get it back. If I didn't, or I told anybody . . . " Kanani shuddered, glancing out at the ocean's blackness.

"I remember when I thought he had threatened me the same way," Josh said as gooseflesh rippled across his shoulders and down his arms.

The doctor arrived. He was short, ruddy-faced, and didn't look as old as Josh's father. However, he took quiet command, briefly asking Kanani questions before taking her down on the elevator to his third-deck office.

Josh suggested to Tank that they walk around until Josh could calm down. They took the outside stairs to the shuffleboard deck, where they saw Micah standing alone.

Josh lowered his voice to Tank. "Don't say anything about what just happened."

They approached Micah, who stood with his back to them, silently contemplating the shuffleboard area.

"Hi," Josh greeted him. "You want to play a game?"

Micah returned the greeting, then shook his head. "No, I was thinking about how scared my grandmother's going to be if they lift her off this place up to a helicopter."

"She's worse?" Josh asked with concern.

"Yes. Ever since the sea got a little rough, she's had a tough time. The doctor said that unless she improves by when we reach American waters, he'll call the Coast Guard and have her flown to a San Diego hospital."

The double glass doors opened so noisily that all three boys turned to look. Kong burst through the doors and headed straight for the boys, but his eyes were fixed on Josh.

"Hey, you dumb haole," he growled, bearing down on Josh like a runaway locomotive. "Kong just see Kanani. She cry, so Kong know you make her do dat. Now you be planty sorry, yeah?"

Josh couldn't believe what he was hearing. He started to explain, but when he opened his mouth, he could make only a croaking sound. Kong reached down with an arm the size of a telephone pole and took hold of Josh's shirt.

Suddenly anger replaced Josh's fear. He leaped up, knocking

Kong's hand off the shirt front. "Now just a minute, Kong!" Josh's voice rose angrily. "I'm tired of you pushing people around, especially me!"

Josh shoved his face close to Kong's so that the big bully drew back. "Listen," Josh continued, his words coming hot and fast, "if it weren't for me, your little sister might be swimming in the Pacific! Now, before you go jumping to conclusions, why don't you find out what really happened?"

Kong took a step back, but Josh moved closer, his face still close to the other boy's.

"Uh . . . ," Kong began uncertainly. "See sistah cry, an' you . . . "

"I didn't make her cry!" Josh exploded in righteous indignation. "Ask Tank! He was there!"

Kong took another step back and glanced at Tank, who quickly retold what had happened. "So Josh is right. If he hadn't rushed in and saved her, you might not have a little sister anymore!"

Kong glanced back at Josh. The fury had ebbed from Josh, and the cold touch of fearful reality returned. He wanted to step back, but forced himself to stand still.

"Uh," Kong said. "Uh . . . " Then, without another word, he turned and rushed back toward the ship's doors.

Josh watched him go before taking a long, slow breath.

"Whew!" Tank whispered in awe. "For a moment, I thought you were a goner. Boy! I never thought I'd see the time when Kong would back down!"

"And I never thought I'd do anything like that," Josh

admitted, sinking weakly into a deck chair. He looked up at Tank and Micah and grinned. "But it sure did feel good!"

Later, after telling Micah they would pray for his grand-mother, Josh and Tank headed for their stateroom.

Tank commented, "I sure hope this means that Kong will never bother us again."

"Me, too, but I sure don't know about him. I've got this strange, uneasy feeling in the pit of my stomach."

"About Kong?"

Josh considered that. "I'm not sure. Maybe that, or Micah's grandmother, or those two men who are after that disk. I just feel real uneasy."

* * *

The next morning the seas were rougher than they had been any time on the trip. But neither Josh nor Tank were bothered by the ship's increasing motion as they sailed north along the Mexican coast.

At the security chief's phoned invitation, Josh joined his father, Tank, Kanani, and her mother in Stark's small, cramped office. None of them was bothered by the slightly rougher seas.

"Here's the latest," the security officer began. "Yount, the suspect who accosted this young lady, didn't return to his stateroom last night, so he's hiding out somewhere on the ship. However, not even a stowaway can escape detection long, so we'll find him."

"Yeah," Tank commented. "Hunger will drive him out."

"Not necessarily," Stark replied. "There's food all over this vessel, day or night. It's all included with the passage, so anyone can eat. Yount won't go hungry."

Tank nodded. "I didn't think of that."

Mr. Ladd asked, "Have you searched every deck?"

"Every one," Stark assured him. "The lowest decks available to passengers are A and B decks. Below that, there are four more for laundry, mechanical, crew quarters, bakery, provisions stores with big walk-in freezers, etcetera, and the engine room lower down. Those are all strictly forbidden to passengers."

Mr. Ladd mused, "So Yount is still somewhere in the passenger part of the ship?"

"He has to be," Stark replied. "The problem is that we have to be very careful in how we conduct our search. We don't want to alert Yount or alarm the other passengers."

"But," Josh said thoughtfully, "Yount obviously doesn't have the disk, so shouldn't you be looking for Tilford?"

"I was coming to that," Stark answered. "The redheaded man obviously has the disk, which he stole from my property room. I've received radio information that the man we know as Tilford is an impostor. He apparently stole the passport and other papers from the real Corby Tilford."

Josh inquired, "Then who's the redheaded man?"

"Real name is Reginald Wallers," Stark explained. "He's a professional industrial spy, just like Yount. Apparently Tilford—or Wallers—wanted to steal the disk in L.A., but Yount beat him to it. There was enough money involved that Wallers followed Yount onto this ship, figuring to take the disk from him and collect the money in Acapulco. You kids messed things up for them."

Josh smiled at Tank and Kanani, who grinned back.

"Unfortunately, however," the security officer continued in an ominous tone, "both those men have a rap sheet* that includes suspicion of homicide."

"You mean murder?" Tank blurted in alarm.

Stark nodded. "Both Wallers and Yount were charged once in separate cases, but neither was ever convicted."

Josh's throat tightened at that frightening news.

Mr. Ladd said, "Far be it from me to suggest anything in your occupation, Mr. Stark, but have you considered the possibility that the real reason you can't find Yount is because the other man, Tilford—rather, Wallers—might have already caused Yount to disappear?"

"I've thought of that. But in the twenty-five years I've sailed on these passenger ships, we've never had a man overboard, accidentally or otherwise. I think Yount is still hiding somewhere. If we don't find him sooner, we'll get him when he goes ashore in Los Angeles. There the harbor authorities will also seize Tilford."

Josh frowned. "But what if something goes wrong? I mean, what if he finds some way to escape from the ship before then?"

Stark explained, "There's no way to do that. One man couldn't lower a lifeboat or tender. We're ten miles off the Baja peninsula, and that's too far to swim."

In the corridor after the meeting, Mrs. Kong looked down

at Josh and gently touched his cheek. "As I told you last night, I am so very grateful to you for risking your life to save my daughter. I just had to tell you again."

Josh was embarrassed, especially when he saw Kanani looking at him with warm, brown eyes. "Thanks," he said.

"My son told me what happened between you two last night. I am sorry for his behavior," Mrs. Kong said.

"It's okay," Josh assured her.

"Nobody ever stood up to him before," Mrs. Kong continued. "I'm not sure how long it will last, but . . . "

"Excuse me," Josh interrupted, turning to Tank. "Look! There goes the redheaded man. He's got a cast on his lower left arm. I wonder what happened?"

"It's not our concern anymore," Tank replied. "Let the security people handle him and Mr. Yount."

"I'm really curious about that cast," Josh said, "so I think I'll find out. You want to come along, Tank?"

"No, thanks! We'll soon arrive safely in Los Angeles, so let's stay away from Tilford."

"He can't do anything to us in daylight," Josh answered.

Without waiting for Tank's reply, Josh started easing through the crowd, trailing the red-haired man.

Chapter Thirteen

A DESPERATE DECISION

Josh managed to follow the man known as Tilford up two flights of stairs and down a corridor toward the casino. Josh stood at the open door, but saw no one. The door at the far end swung slightly, as if someone had just walked through it. Josh was reluctant to pass through the glitzy gaming area of roulette wheels, slot machines, and other gambling devices. He had never seen them before, but his father had told him that such facilities were common on seagoing passenger ships.

Josh started to turn around just as the door on the far end of the room opened and the red-haired man stepped through. Josh gulped as Tilford walked toward him, the white cast prominent on his left forearm.

"Why are you following me, kid?" he demanded roughly.

"Uh . . . ," Josh stammered, backing up a step.

"You don't need to answer," Tilford said in a more moderate tone. He crossed in front of a blackjack table and stopped in front of Josh. "I know why. I must say you've got more nerve than most kids your age."

"I . . . ," Josh said, floundering for the right words.

"You a gambler?" the man asked. When Josh shook his head, Tilford continued, "I am. In fact, I'm betting a hundred thousand dollars on the success of this trip. That's a lot of money, isn't it?"

"Sure is."

"A gambler has to have confidence; otherwise, he'd never risk anything. Right now, I'm so sure that I'm going to win this game that I'll tell you something. Nobody is going to stop me; not you, not Yount, not the security officers or even the cops who will be waiting for me when we dock in Los Angeles."

Josh frowned, and Tilford explained, "I'm telling you this because that's part of the thrill of gambling. And to make it more exciting, I'm going to tell you that I'll not only walk away with the hundred grand, but I'll have a laugh at everybody's efforts to stop me. Having you know this adds to the sense of risk."

Josh still frowned, not understanding.

Tilford continued, "Too bad we can't meet afterward so you can see how I did it. Oh, well. See you around."

Josh watched the red-haired man walk away whistling. Then Josh hurried to Tank and breathlessly told him what Tilford had said. The two boys then told Mr. Ladd, and all three reported to Dave Stark.

The security supervisor commented, "Yes, my officers have already reported the incident to me, but thanks for coming to me, because Tilford is wrong. He's a cool one, but there is no way he can get off this ship without getting caught.

Neither can Yount."

"Speaking of Yount," Mr. Ladd said, "have you found any sign of him?"

"Not yet. Nobody except Kanani has seen him without his beard, and he somehow escaped having his picture taken on this cruise, so we don't even have a photo. But we still have a day at sea to find him."

Josh commented, "Yount must also know that someone is willing to pay a hundred thousand dollars for that disk. Remember, he told Kanani he was desperate to recover it. If he finds out that Tilford has it . . . "

"Even if Yount does," the security officer broke in, "neither man is going to get off this ship with that disk. Even if they had an accomplice, our surveillance would disclose that, and we'll watch that person, too."

Stark looked at Josh, saying, "It's too bad you couldn't have bet with Tilford, because he's going to lose his bet, and he won't be laughing when he does."

Afterward, when the two boys walked along the promenade deck, Josh was troubled.

"We're all overlooking something," he mused thoughtfully. "I just wish we could figure it out."

"Just be grateful that nobody has been thrown overboard by either of those men," Tank replied. "With that kind of money at stake, they're not going to let us get in the way." He glanced around before adding, "So it's a good thing security people are watching us, but it's a little spooky to think of anyone doing that."

Both boys were skittish, but nothing happened the rest of that day.

That evening, their last at sea, everyone kept only a small hand-carried piece of luggage. They packed all their other bags and set them outside their cabin doors for the porters.

Josh looked thoughtfully at his bag, thinking how much adventure had come out of it. *And it may not be over,* he warned himself. *We're still several hours from Los Angeles.*

* * *

When Josh awoke shortly after dawn, he was surprised to see that Tank was already dressed.

"Couldn't sleep," Tank confessed. "I kept expecting something unexpected to happen. But if we make it safely through the next few hours, it'll all be over."

"I wish we could see the police grab the redheaded man and recover that disk," Josh said, sitting up. "I'll get dressed, and we can have our last breakfast on deck."

"Last breakfast?" Tank croaked. "Don't say that!"

* * *

The air was warm and pleasant as the boys waited in line to place their orders. Josh looked off to the side and saw that the seas were still running a little high with occasional white-caps. *I'm glad that I never had any sign of seasickness,* he told himself.

Tank, standing in front of Josh, turned to say, "I wonder how Micah's grandmother is doing?"

Before Josh could answer, Kong came on deck and headed straight for Josh and Tank.

"Oh no!" Tank exclaimed under his breath. "He's going to spoil our last day at sea!"

The big bully marched up to Josh and Tank and stopped, looking hard at them. Josh waited, hoping that Kong wouldn't make a scene in front of everybody.

"Hey, you haole boys," Kong said, "Kong want talk."

He turned away and walked toward a vacant white table at the port rail. He sat down, then motioned for Josh and Tank, who still stood uncertainly in the food line.

"Well," Josh said with a sigh, "we may as well face up to whatever he's got in mind."

When the friends had taken chairs opposite Kong, he leaned massive elbows on the table and spoke across it. "Kong think long time," he began. "Not you' fault you got fathahs and Kong don't. Den you both save da kine Kong sistah. You good guys—foh haoles."

"Thanks," Josh replied, glancing at Tank, who raised his eyebrows as though he meant he also wasn't sure where Kong was going with his thoughts. However, it didn't sound as though he planned to thump on them.

"Kong say mahalo to you, too," he said, then lowered his eyes and squirmed. "You tell Kong somethin'. If you do something bad, maybe like tell lie, you t'ink maybe so you tell da fathah?"

Josh hesitated, fearing some kind of a trap, so he looked at Tank. When he nodded, Josh did the same. "Yes, Kong. It wouldn't be easy, but that would be the right thing, so we'd tell our fathers."

"Even maybe so you get da kine . . . uh . . . punish?"

"Even if we were disciplined," Josh replied.

The big boy sat in silence for a long moment, then abruptly stood. "Mahalo," he said briskly, and left.

Tank stared after him. "What do you suppose that was all about?"

"I don't know, but I'm glad we've still got our teeth. Come on, let's get back in that food line."

They discussed Kong's strange behavior while they heaped their plates with delicious-smelling food and found a table near the stern rail.

Tank observed, "The ship's not making much of a wake today. See? Usually it stretches out a half mile or so behind us. I wonder why?"

Josh stared thoughtfully at the diminished white trail before answering. "I think we're slowing down."

"Can't be. We're nowhere near land, and we're not supposed to reach Los Angeles until noon."

Josh shrugged and seated himself. "Well, I guess it doesn't concern us." He started to close his eyes to ask a silent blessing, then sat up abruptly. "Be right back."

Josh hurried to where he could look down on the part of the ship's deck where shuffleboard games were played. This area extended farther aft than any other part of the vessel. Crewmen hurriedly removed strings of electric lights, other overhead obstructions, and deck chairs.

Tank joined Josh, asking, "What're they doing?"

"I hope I'm wrong, but I think they're getting ready for a

Coast Guard helicopter."

"Micah's grandmother!" Tank exclaimed.

The boys forgot their food. They hurried off the deck and down the outside stairs to be with Micah.

He stood near the superstructure, watching a gurney* being wheeled out onto the shuffleboard area by two security officers. The doctor and a uniformed nurse followed a patient covered with a light blanket from feet to neck.

Micah shaded his eyes against the sun's glare and looked up at the sky as Josh and Tank reached him.

"I'm sorry," Josh said, lightly touching Micah on the shoulder.

"Huh?" Micah asked, lowering his gaze to the boys.

"Your grandmother," Josh explained. "We're sorry."

Micah stared at them. "What are you talking about?"

Josh heard the approaching beat of a big helicopter as he replied, "How bad is she?"

"Who? Grandma? She's getting dressed to go home."

"What?" Tank exclaimed, then glanced toward the gurney. "Then who's on that?"

Micah shrugged. "Search me. I was just standing here when all this started happening."

Tank mused, "Then it's somebody else who got really sick and can't wait for us to reach port, I guess."

Josh didn't say anything, but watched the helicopter with its distinctive orange stripe on a white fuselage as it slowed above the barely moving ship.

There had been no announcement on the public-address

system. Josh guessed that the captain had chosen not to alarm the other passengers by calling attention to the unusual activity. Only those outside would know about the helicopter. Josh saw that all passengers on the decks were watching the chopper.

Alarm bells suddenly began clanging in Josh's mind. He dashed across the deck to the doctor. "Remember me?" he asked. "Josh Ladd. You helped with the girl . . . "

"I remember," the doctor replied as Tank and Micah joined them.

"Who's that?" Josh asked, pointing to the person on the gurney.

"A very sick patient. Had some sort of virulent attack in the night. I've done all I can for him, but he needs immediate medical assistance I'm not equipped to render."

Josh's voice rose in excitement. "Is his name Corby Tilford?"

The doctor nodded. "A friend of yours?"

Josh evaded the question while his mind leaped away in wild thoughts. "Does he have anything with him?"

"Only a surgical gown under that blanket."

Josh recalled the hated gowns he sometimes had to wear when having a physical exam. It was a sacklike garment without pockets that opened down the back and made modesty a near impossibility. There was no way anything could be carried in that gown, yet the jangling alarms continued inside Josh's head.

The helicopter hovered directly overhead, the rotary blades

causing a severe downdraft that made Josh and the others turn away to shield their eyes.

The doctor raised his voice to be heard over the sound of the chopper. "Would you boys mind stepping back out of the way?"

Tank and Micah retreated, but Josh hesitated. He glanced up at the hovering helicopter. A helmeted crewman started lowering a metal cable with a kind of long, narrow wire basket suspended from the end.

"Doctor," Josh shouted, "when did you put a cast on his arm?"

"I didn't. He already had it last night when I saw him for the first time after he called for my help. Now, please step over there with your friends."

Josh rejoined them, saying to Tank, "He's getting away with the disk!"

"What?" Tank cried in disbelief. "That man's so sick he can't move, and you think he's stealing something."

"Tilford told me that he's betting a hundred thousand dollars that he gets off this ship with that disk. I think he planned this whole thing, including taking something last night that made him seem real sick but isn't really serious."

"Your imagination is running away with you! Even if he had the disk, you heard the doctor. There's no way he could hide something like that the way he is now. If he tried, the doctor would have seen it."

Josh glanced toward the still form on the gurney as the metal basket was slowly lowered from the chopper.

"I guess you're right, Tank," he admitted with a sigh.

Dave Stark, in uniform, came hurrying across the deck, heading for the spot where the patient waited.

The helicopter's downdraft tore loose one corner of the blanket. The nurse grabbed it and readjusted it about the patient where his left arm had been briefly exposed. Josh stared and then suddenly jerked as though he'd been hit by an electric shock. *That's it!* he thought wildly. Then doubt immediately assailed him and he hesitated, fearful that he might be wrong. He faced a terrible decision.

What should I do? he anguished silently. *If I say something, and I'm wrong, everybody will laugh at me. So the easiest thing is to keep quiet. But if I'm right, and I don't say anything, Tilford will get away with it.*

With a quick, silent prayer for guidance, Josh turned to Tank and began, "I think . . . " Then Josh broke off abruptly and made his decision with all its risks.

He turned and ran to intercept the chief security officer. "Mr. Stark, wait!"

Stark replied brusquely, "Please stay back, Josh."

"In a minute," Josh replied. "But first, please listen to me! That's Mr. Tilford over there, and I'm sure he's trying to get away with the stolen disk."

Stark said, "I know it's Tilford. I personally checked him when the doctor wanted to call the Coast Guard. Getting sick fouled up Tilford's plans to get off the ship with the disk."

Josh cupped his hands to be heard above the noise of the helicopter's whirling blades and noisy motor. "But he could have hidden the disk on him *before* he got sick."

"Not a chance, Josh. My officer who had Tilford under surveillance last night called me when he became sick. That surveillance has continued to this moment. There's no way he could hide that disk or anything else."

"Please! Look at the cast on his arm."

"There's no need because the doctor would have seen the disk when he put the cast on."

In dismay, Josh glanced over to where the ship's uniformed officers waited with upstretched arms as the basket neared them. Desperately, Josh looked back at Stark. "The doctor didn't put that cast on!"

"What?" Stark exclaimed as the patient was transferred from the gurney to the dangling basket.

Josh nodded vehemently. "That's what he told me a minute ago. Mr. Tilford was already wearing the cast *before* he got sick. I saw it yesterday, too."

"You sure, Josh?"

"Yes! Please at least take a look!" Josh yelled as those around the gurney stepped back and looked up.

The doctor raised his right arm and jerked his thumb upward, signaling the chopper crewman overhead to begin lifting the patient.

Stark ran toward the helicopter and shouted, "Hey, Doc! Hold it a minute!"

He waved his open hands toward the overhead crewman, and the cable stopped.

The security chief stepped to the litter and reached under

the blanket. Josh held his breath while the doctor, the nurse, and two other security men joined Stark. They blocked the boy's view, but a moment later they stepped back.

Stark turned around and held up two pieces of a cast. In his other hand, he displayed a small disk. He called, "You were right, Josh!"

After the patient was safely inside the helicopter and it had flown off, Josh, Tank, and Micah hurried to where Stark was huddled with the doctor, nurse, and other security officers.

Stark showed the cast to the three boys. "It's made in two pieces with a hidden latch and hinge so it can be slipped off and on. See there inside the part that goes over the inner forearm? There's a special indentation created where the disk was hidden. But how did you guess that, Josh?"

He shrugged. "It was the only possible hiding place, so I took a chance."

"You're a pretty bright boy," Stark said. "Well, I'd better go radio ahead so that authorities can arrest Tilford when he reaches the hospital." Stark started to turn away, then looked back at Josh with a grin. "You should have seen his face when I took that cast off and found the disk."

Josh replied, "I'd rather hear what he says when he finds that he lost his hundred-thousand-dollar gamble."

* * *

After saying a friendly good-bye to Vicki and her mother at dockside, Josh and the others took the bus to Los Angeles International Airport to wait for their flight to Honolulu.

There Kanani came over to Josh. She smiled shyly at him.

"Thanks to what you said to my brother, he's changed. He confessed to your dad that I really drew the picture that won the cruise."

"So I heard," Josh replied, wondering if Kong had really changed.

"Kamuela said he was willing to make it up to your dad for telling that lie. That surprised me."

"That's good," Josh answered.

"And if it weren't for you," Kanani added, a tremor in her voice, "Mr. Yount might have thrown me overboard."

"I think he was just trying to scare you. Anyway, they caught him trying to leave the ship, so he's in jail."

"Is it true that he just slept on deck after shaving off his beard, and sort of stowed away in plain sight?"

"That's what Mr. Stark told me."

Kanani's voice grew soft. "Josh, I want you to know that this experience has made me learn to control my imagination. It got me into lots of trouble."

Josh smiled at her. "I learned something out of this, too. At first I made some wrong decisions, but when it really counted, I remembered the proper way is to trust God and not depend on my own understanding*."

"You also solved a mystery and found out how to get along with a difficult person like my brother, and in hard circumstances, too. So it's been a good cruise."

"Yes, it has—a really good one," Josh agreed.

He and Kanani happily walked back together to join the others for their flight to Hawaii.

GLOSSARY

CHAPTER 1

Kamuela (kah-muh-way-LAH): Hawaiian for "Samuel."

Muumuu (MOO-oo-MOO-oo): A loose, colorful dress or gown worn by women in Hawaii. This word is sometimes mispronounced "moo-moo."

Waikiki (WHY-Kee-KEE): Honolulu's tourist district, which encompasses Hawaii's most famous white-sand-beach. Waikiki is Hawaiian for "spouting water."

Honolulu (hoe-no-LOO-LOO): Hawaii's capital and the most populous city in the fiftieth state; located on the island of Oahu. In Hawaiian, Honolulu means "sheltered bay."

Haole (HOW-lee): A Hawaiian word originally meaning "stranger," but now used to mean "Caucasian," or "white person."

Holo holo (HOE-lo HOE-lo): Commonly used to mean "go for a walk," but it also means "ride," "sail," etc.

Da kine (dah-kine): Pidgin English for "the kind." This is an expression not usually translated literally.

Pidgin English (PIDJ-uhn): A simplified version of English. It was originally used in the Orient for communication between people who spoke different languages.

Promenade deck: A passenger vessel's deck used for strolling or exercise.

Malihinis (mah-lah-HEE-nees): Hawaiian for "newcomers."

CHAPTER 2
Sistah (sis-TAH): Pidgin for "sister."

Maître d' (may-tre dee): Short for the French term *maître d'hôtel*, meaning "head waiter," "steward," or "manager."

CHAPTER 3
Port: The left side of a vessel or aircraft, facing forward.

Bow: The forward part of a ship.

Escargot (S-KAR-go): French for an edible snail, a gourmet delicacy.

Caviar (khah-vee-are): The roe (or eggs) of a large fish (such as sturgeon) and usually served as an appetizer.

Mahalo (mah-HA-lo): Hawaiian for "thanks."

CHAPTER 4
Kajiwara (Kah-gee-WHAR-ah): A Japanese surname.

Pupule (poo-POO-lay): Hawaiian for "crazy."

Heli mai (HAY-lee my): Hawaiian for "come here."

Stern: The after part or rear of a vessel.

CHAPTER 5

Puerto Vallarta (Pwer-toe VAL-yar-TAH): A scenic, intriguing Pacific port in Mexico that is popular with American visitors.

Starboard: The right side of a vessel or aircraft, facing forward.

Baja peninsula (bah-HAH pen-in-soo-LAH): The long, narrow strip of land extending from the southern tip of California deep into Mexico.

CHAPTER 6

Shoulder boards: Boardlike emblems worn on the shoulders of uniforms to designate rank or duty.

Zihuatenejo (Zee-whah-teh-nay-HO): A rustic, sleepy but delightful little community with fine beaches and tropical scenery on Mexico's Pacific shore.

Acapulco (ah-kah-POOL-koe): A renowned Mexican resort with modern high-rise buildings overlooking a quaint old section of town dating back to the days when it was a fishing village.

CHAPTER 7

Planty (PLANT-ee): Pidgin for "plenty."

CHAPTER 8

Gringo (GRING-go): Spanish for "stranger."

Sombrero (som-BREH-oh): A Spanish term for a wide-brimmed men's hat.

Makua kane (mah-coo-AH khan-EE): Hawaiian for "male

parent," or "father."

Keike kane (KAY-kee khan-EE): Hawaiian for "male child," or "boy."

Huhu (HOO-hoo): Hawaiian for "angry."

Pilikia (pee-lee-KEE-ah): Hawaiian for "trouble."

Wahine (wah-HEE-nee): Hawaiian for "female."

Buenos tardes (bway-nos tar-days): Spanish for "good afternoon."

CHAPTER 9

Guadalupe (Gwa-dah-loo-PAY): In the 1500s, an Indian reported a vision of the Virgin Mary at a place in Mexico that was renamed for the shrine in Spain honoring Our Lady of Guadalupe.

CHAPTER 10

Cover: A false name or story used to protect someone.

Gracias (GRAH-see-us): Spanish for "thanks."

You got stink ear: Pidgin for "you don't listen well."

CHAPTER 11

Alto (AHL-toe): Spanish for "halt."

Policia (poe-LEE-cee-ah): Spanish for "police."

CHAPTER 12

Rap sheet: The informal term for a criminal record kept on individual law-breakers.

CHAPTER 13

Gurney: A wheeled cart used as a stretcher to move patients, as in a hospital.

Own understanding: The reference is from Proverbs 3:5-6. "Trust in the Lord with all your heart and lean not on your own understanding; in all your ways acknowledge him, and he will make your paths straight" (NIV).

Caution! Danger and Surprises Ahead!

Twist your way through a maze of mystery and thrills. Twelve-year-old Josh Ladd always seems to end up in the middle of risky situations, and *you* can join him and his family in each sensational story of the *Ladd Family Adventure* series. Each hard-to-put-down paperback combines nonstop action and intrigue with unforgettable lessons about trusting God.

Night of the Vanishing Lights
Josh tries to solve the mystery at a Hawaiian temple and runs into a series of adventures on land and under water.

Eye of the Hurricane
Josh and Tank race against time and a dangerous storm in search of Josh's father.

Terror at Forbidden Falls
Josh and his friends uncover a dangerous plot to detonate a nuclear device in Honolulu.

Peril at Pirate's Point
When Josh and Tank try to get help for Tank's injured father, they're captured by a pair of dangerous smugglers.

Mystery of the Wild Surfer
A young surfer saves Josh from drowning off the coast of Hawaii. But when Josh tries to befriend him, he and his family are threatened by dangerous men.

Secret of the Sunken Sub
A fun-filled fishing trip takes a perilous turn when Josh witnesses the sinking of a Soviet robot submarine and is pursued by Russian spies.

The Dangerous Canoe Race
Josh and his friends are swept into adventure when they are challenged to an outrigger canoe race by a bully who will do anything to win.

Mystery of the Island Jungle
Josh must find the courage to free his friend from a vicious stranger.

The Legend of Fire
Josh attempts to rescue his father from kidnappers and an erupting volcano.

Secret of the Shark Pit
The Ladds brave a life-or-death race for hidden treasure.

Available at your local Christian bookstore.

Breakaway

With colorful graphics, hot topics, and humor, this magazine for teen guys helps them keep their faith on course *and* gives the latest info on sports, music, celebrities . . . even girls. Best of all, this publication shows teens how they can put their Christian faith into practice and resist peer pressure.

All magazines are published monthly except where otherwise noted. For more information regarding these and other resources, please call Focus on the Family at (719) 531-5181, or write to us at Focus on the Family, Colorado Springs, CO 80995.